second kiss

A NOVEL

NATALIE PALMER

second kiss

A NOVEL

TATE PUBLISHING *& Enterprises*

Published by Tate Publishing & Enterprises, LLC
127 E. Trade Center Terrace | Mustang, Oklahoma 73064 USA
1.888.361.9473 | www.tatepublishing.com

Tate Publishing is committed to excellence in the publishing industry. The company reflects the philosophy established by the founders, based on Psalm 68:11,
"The Lord gave the word and great was the company of those who published it."

Book design copyright © 2010 by Tate Publishing, LLC. All rights reserved.
Cover design by Kellie Southerland
Interior design by Jeff Fisher

Published in the United States of America

ISBN:978-1-61663-767-5
1. Fiction, Coming of Age
2. Fiction, Romance, Contemporary
10.08.31

For James –

my best friend (and secretly more)

chapter one

I shut my eyes and winced in pain as a bright light flashed across my face. I was surrounded by a crowd of kids who were all pointing, whispering, and shooting photographs. I looked down to find in my own hands an old, dusty camera. It was the old-fashioned Polaroid kind where your picture automatically comes sliding through the slot. I lifted the camera to my eye, and standing in the center of my peephole was Trace Weston. My stomach fluttered when his eyes locked with mine. I couldn't believe that even in my dreams Trace Weston gave me butterflies. His perfect blue eyes pinched together slightly. They were full of question and intrigue. I flexed my finger and felt a click. The camera flashed, and Trace buckled over and covered his face with both arms. The crowd around me gasped. I stood up straight, scanning my audience. Faces familiar, and some that were new, winced in embarrassment. "Why'd you do it, Gemma?" The voice from behind me was low, collected, and female. I tried to turn around and see who belonged to the unfamiliar voice, but

I couldn't move. The camera in my hands groaned as the photo paper rolled out from its holster. I waved the picture in the air, waiting for Trace to appear. But when the colors came into focus, it wasn't a photo of Trace at all. The person that slowly appeared in my hands was someone who meant much more to me than a silly little crush. He was someone who knew me better than I knew myself. And someone whom I loved inside and out. The boy in the photo was Jess.

Crack! I was awakened by a sharp object hitting against the glass of my bedroom window. I rubbed my eyes and blinked in the darkness at my clock. It was almost midnight. I rolled out of bed and grabbed my coat that was hanging on the closet door. I flipped the overhead light on and then off again just as quickly. That was the signal that I was awake and on my way.

By the time I made it downstairs and out my back door, Jess was sitting on my porch steps with his head resting in both hands.

"Your dad?" I said after I closed the door.

Jess jerked around to look at me. "Were you asleep?"

I sat next to him on the step. "I don't mind. I was dreaming weird tonight."

Jess rubbed his hand over his exhausted eyes. "My dad lost his job."

I cringed. Jess was a slightly shorter, better-looking, and much thinner replica of his father. But their personalities couldn't be more different. While Jess never thought about himself, his father thought about nobody *but* himself. And as soft spoken and kind as Jess was, so his father was loud, abrupt, and downright mean.

Jess had started coming to my window at night when his dad first began drinking. And now, six years later, Jess was sitting in his usual spot on my back porch, still trying to escape him.

"Not again," I groaned as I thought about how many times his dad had lost his job. He always drank more after getting fired.

Jess hadn't said much since I joined him on the steps, but this wasn't unusual. On nights like this I was the one doing all the talking. Jess didn't want to acknowledge what was going on at his house. But he couldn't bring himself to talk about anything of less importance either. He smiled as I rambled on about my day, telling him things that were inconsequential enough to not have been brought up on our walk home from school, but things that now—at the late hour—seemed hilarious. Somewhere in the middle of all my chatter I went inside and got us some hot chocolate. It was the early part of February, and the grass beyond our porch was still covered in gray snow.

Jess held the yellow mug of hot chocolate up to his face, letting the steam sweep around his cheeks. "So what was your dream about?"

I took a sip of my hot chocolate as I tried to recall the dream. Images of the Polaroid camera and Trace Weston skipped around in my brain. I shook my head at the memory. "It was about Trace. I did something stupid in fifth period today, and I can't seem to get it out of my head." I poked at the chunks of unmixed chocolate powder in my mug. "I'm surprised I forgot to tell you about this earlier."

Jess set his mug down and leaned back on his hands. "I'm glad you saved it. I need a good laugh tonight."

"Well, I took my camera to school today because I needed it for my photography class. We had a pop quiz in the class before, and I finished early. So I took out my camera to make sure it was working."

Jess puffed out his bottom lip. "So far not too stupid."

"Just wait," I moaned. "Trace Weston sits in the row next to me and one seat up in that class."

"Ah, Trace." Jess nodded his head with exaggeration. "So what happened?"

"Well, my camera wouldn't turn on, so I got nervous because we had to have it all ready for my photography class. So I'm pushing all the buttons on my camera, trying to figure out what's wrong." I moved my hands and fingers in a mime as though I had the camera in my hand at that moment. "Next thing I know, the camera is on and I'm accidentally taking a picture! The flash went off and everything!"

"So?" Jess shrugged his shoulders as though asking, *What's the big deal?*

"The camera was in my lap, but when it flashed it was pointed directly at Trace. The whole class saw it. They were all making jokes about how I'm stalking him and was secretly taking his picture!"

Jess watched me with humored eyes as I reenacted the whole scene. As horrible as it all seemed during fifth period, it was something I could laugh about now. Because even my most humiliating moments seemed funny somehow when I told them to Jess.

Jess was trying to conceal a smile. "Well there was one good thing that came from it."

I looked at him with one eyebrow raised. "Yeah, what's that?"

"You got a picture of the guy you like. Now you can put it in your journal and look at it every night." His eyes were full of humor as he took another sip from his mug. "Isn't that what girls like to do?"

I let my head fall into my hands. "I flipped through my pictures after class to see if I had at least gotten a good shot of him. All I have to show for it is a fuzzy picture of Trace Weston's knee."

Jess pushed himself to standing then turned to help me up as well. "I'm sure you could sell it on eBay. There are probably a thousand girls who would give their allowance for a picture of Trace Weston's knee." Jess laughed softly at his joke, and I could tell he was happier now than when he had come. "Thanks for coming down," he spoke quietly. "I always feel better after we've talked."

"I'm glad that my humiliating experiences lift your spirits," I said playfully. Then I lowered my head and asked, "Are you going to be okay?"

But of course Jess never liked the attention on him so he replied, "The question is, are *you* going to be okay?" He began walking away from the deck, leaving me standing alone with my arms hugging my waist. His words were fading as he joked, "If you want to stalk somebody you should really learn *not* to do it in the middle of a full classroom." He waved goodbye with one hand held high above his head as he disappeared at the side of my house. And then he was gone, and I felt cold for the first time since I stepped outside.

chapter two

Jess came early the next morning to pick me up for school. He had been walking me to school since I started kindergarten. My sister, Bridget, was three years older than me, but she always went to charter schools, so my mom's best friend, Caris, from across the street offered her son to walk me to school. We had been walking to school and back together ever since.

Jess really didn't need to walk me to school anymore since I was fourteen and would probably beat someone up before he would. But over the years he became my best friend. I felt proud walking to school with Jess. He was tall and confident, and he looked older than a fifteen-year-old. Sometimes people asked me if he was my boyfriend. Of course he wasn't. Jess didn't date in junior high. Neither did I, but that was because I was terrified of talking to boys (except Jess of course). Jess didn't date because it was one of his rules.

"Rule number three," Jess had announced on a walk home from school last year. He was trying to decipher his hand writing that he had scribbled on a crumpled piece of lined paper during seventh period. The first two rules he had made for himself were: no drinking from the school drinking fountains—which was entirely understandable—and never pass gas in public—to which I was particularly grateful. But his third rule was anything but acceptable.

"No dating," he had read aloud with his chin high and a voice full of dignity.

"Ever?" I moaned.

Jess squinted his eyes toward the clouds. "No, not *ever*. I'll start dating when I'm a junior in high school." He made the addendum to his list with a pen he had fetched from behind his ear.

"Great," I grumbled. "You are going to be a complete loser for the next two years."

Jess shrugged. "I don't care."

And he really didn't.

Jess and I talked a lot. We had a half mile walk to and from school every day to talk about whatever we wanted. When he was walking me to school for the first time, my first question to him was why his parents gave him a girl's name. I knew a girl named Jessica, whose mom called her Jess for short. Jess had said that his name was Kevin Jessop Tyler. It was a name that had been handed down from generation to generation for a gazillion generations. But since his dad's name was Kevin, he went by Jessop. No one ever called him Jessop though, just Jess.

My name is Gemmalynn Judith Mitchell. Like Jess, no one called me by my full first name except for teachers on the first day of class, or my grandmother, who insisted on calling me the full Gemmalynn Judith every time she saw me, along with squeezing what was left of the skin on my cheeks between her cold, leathery fingers.

But to everyone else and to myself, I was Gemma. I was born in a small town nestled in the center of the Nantahala National Forest in Western North Carolina. Our town is called Franklin, or "The Gem Capital of the World." I'm sure a few hundred years ago that was a pretty cool thing. But these days people just order their gems over the Internet. They don't really care where they come from. But, as an obvious conclusion, that's how I got my name, Gemma.

Jess and I were done discussing the basics, like names and favorite pizza flavors, by the time I was three weeks into kindergarten. So we told each other stories and embarrassing moments, plans for when we grew up and places we wanted to visit someday.

And now, nearly ten years later, he was still holding the door for me as we both made our way into school. Valentine's Day was only a week away, and as we walked through the halls we were bombarded with pink balloons and cutout paper hearts that dangled from the ceiling and walls. Jess was a year older than me in school, so he told me to have a good day as he turned down the ninth grade hall, leaving me to fend for myself through seven torturous periods. Even through the pinkish mess I eventually found my locker—which actually wasn't my locker at all. Since I was eight my family had been taking a yearly vacation to Cape

Cod. Every year our timeshare fell on the same week as school registration. Because I registered late I always got the worst pick for my locker location. This year I was assigned to the seventh grade hall. I was in eighth grade and wouldn't be caught dead hanging around a bunch of seventh graders, so luckily, my friend Nina Riley let me share hers. Nina was a genius. Ninety-nine point nine percent of the conversations she had with people were about chemistry, and yet she was somehow graceful and undeniably beautiful at the same time. All the boys liked her, but most of them were too scared to approach her. Clarissa had the locker next to us. She was pretty too, but she tried too hard to look older than she was. She didn't care much about school, but she never missed a day to avoid being behind on any of the gossip.

"I have my first zit!" Clarissa exclaimed as she twisted the lock on her locker. For those of us—me—who were impatiently waiting for any sign of maturation to hit their frail, childish body, I felt anything but bad for her. Clarissa had started her "woman cycles," as my mom disgustingly called them, last year. She was one of the first girls in our grade to "start." I was one of the last girls in our grade to have "not started." I didn't even need a bra. Sometimes I wondered if something was wrong with me. Even though I didn't *need* a bra, my mom still bought me a little white "training" bra at Kmart a couple months ago. The first day I wore it I had felt like I was walking around all day with bandages across my chest. I had felt like the whole world knew that I was wearing this new piece of underwear with white and pink bows, and they all knew that I was faking it.

Clarissa opened her locker and peered into the mini mirror that was hanging from the inside of her locker door.

Nina walked up to the lockers just in time. "Don't pop it, Clarissa! I read in a book once that the puss spreads and makes you break out more." Nina and Clarissa had instantly become best friends on the first day of school. I attributed it to the fact that they both could have passed as tenth graders; Nina for her intelligence and Clarissa for her body shape. I retrieved my history book that I had thrown on the top shelf the day before. I secretly glanced toward Clarissa—who was viewing her face from four different angles—and wondered how it would feel to actually have a need for a mirror in my locker. There wasn't much that I could alter with my boring, brown ponytail and make-up-less complexion. Clarissa batted her eyes in the mirror as I sighed and walked toward my first class. I was ten feet down the hall when Clarissa suddenly realized that a world existed beyond her face.

"Hey, Gemma! Are you going to the Valentine's dance on Friday?" Of course I was going to the dance. It was during school hours, and you needed a note from your parents to be excused. I told her this matter-of-factly before she responded with an annoyingly flirtatious voice, "Are you going to ask Trace Weston to dance?" It had been a huge mistake to tell Clarissa about my crush. She had caught me off guard one day between fourth and fifth period. She had asked me so blatantly who I liked that I didn't know what to do but tell her the truth. I had regretted it ever since.

I scowled at Clarissa. "No! I would never ask him to dance. Just because I kind of like him," not completely accurate, "doesn't mean I want to dance with him!" It was true. Sure, I thought Trace was the most perfect male to walk the face of the planet. And true, I got crazy butterflies in my stomach whenever he was within twenty feet of me. But the thought of talking to him or—even worse—*dancing* with him made me sick to my stomach.

Nina and Clarissa followed close behind me. "Gemma!" they yelled over the crowded hall. "You *have* to ask him to dance! You just *have* to!"

I ignored them and walked faster through the maze of students lining the hall. "Gemma!" they continued. I couldn't separate who was saying what, they sounded so alike. "What do you have to lose? It's Valentine's Day!" I kept walking as I yell-whispered to them over my shoulder that I had everything to lose! Especially my dignity! Then Clarissa said the unexpected. "If you ask Trace Weston," she provided a dramatic pause, "then I'll ask Jess Tyler." My feet came to a screeching halt. I didn't mean to be so dramatic, but her proposition was huge! And unpredictable. Clarissa ask Jess to dance? Was she serious? Clarissa and Nina caught up to me and crunched in so close at my sides that the three of us formed a blockade in the middle of the hall. I stared seriously into Clarissa's overly mature face and whispered in a low, dangerous tone, "You swear?" Clarissa raised one corner of her mouth into a mysterious grin and nodded her head only once. We shook hands and the deal was done.

We agreed to meet at lunch—as if we didn't eat lunch together every day—to discuss our dance plans. First, second, third, and fourth periods crawled on as I anticipated the Valentine's dance discussion. I found myself daydreaming in history class more over Jess and Clarissa than Trace and me. I knew that it was my mission in life to get Jess and Clarissa together ever since Jess told me on the first day of school that year that he thought she was cute. He would get angry at me when I would bring it up, though, insisting that he had said it to be nice, but he hadn't thought about her since.

I was convinced otherwise.

It made perfect sense in my mind. Jess was old, and Clarissa *looked* old. I had asked Clarissa once if she liked Jess. She had giggled for about five minutes before exclaiming that he was a ninth grader and she didn't date ninth graders.

"Besides," she had said the first (and last) night that Clarissa and Nina came to my house for a sleepover, "I like Joseph Horton because he wears a leather coat." Clarissa *would* like someone for something so stupid.

But now she had agreed to ask Jess to dance. It was going to be the dance that would be sure to make Jess the happiest boy in the world.

I reached the long yellow-gold lunch table and straddled the awkward bench. I set down my brown plastic tray that was balancing my wobbly plate of spaghetti and meat sauce, breadstick, and a chocolate milk. I couldn't understand those girls who insisted on just sprinkling cheese over plain noodles as though they were too cool to eat cafeteria meat sauce. I should have reminded them that they were already committing social suicide for ordering cafeteria food in the first place.

Clarissa and Nina were at the table when I arrived— Nina with her own plate of spaghetti and Clarissa with her apple. Who did she think she was eating just an apple for lunch? It made me reconsider our dance plans. I wasn't sure that I wanted Jess dancing with a girl with such ridiculous eating habits.

I twirled my first bite of noodles around my fork as Clarissa bombarded me with her internal thoughts. "Okay," she began, "this is going to be the best dance ever! Not only are you going to dance with Trace, but Nina and I have decided that we're going to find out if he likes you!" My mouth was full of noodles and meat sauce, making it impossible for me to respond. I shook my head a hundred miles per hour with my eyes wide open until I had a chance to swallow.

"Absolutely not!" I yelled as little pieces of noodle spewed from my mouth. Clarissa seemed satisfied that I was so distraught with the idea.

"Do you want me to ask Jess to dance or not?" she threatened.

"Not!" I yelled back. "Who eats just an apple for lunch anyway?"

Clarissa was obviously stunned by my ease at releasing her from the contract. She waved the apple in front of my face in defense. "I had a huge breakfast! I'm not hungry!"

I sighed and looked around the cafeteria for another group of girls I could try to become friends with. Everyone looked so settled in their "groups." No room for a nerdy, hot lunch-eating eighth grader who didn't even need a bra. Clarissa could have easily blended into another group. She had all the traits of the cool kids; the apple for lunch, and of course the zit. Nina could have probably branched out as well. She was just too comfortable with us.

"You don't have to do a thing!" It was Nina's voice this time, and I was surprised that she was this involved in the planning. I was too stunned to talk, so Nina continued. "We're going to do all the work; we'll talk to him, we'll tell him that you like him, and that if he likes you back he should ask you to dance."

"The last dance!" Clarissa blurted out. She raised her eyebrows and took a big bite out of her apple. I had to think about this. Everyone knew that the last dance was the most important dance. You could dance to every other slow song, but the boy with whom you danced the *last* dance—was your truest of all true loves. It was like the first kiss. The first kiss and the last dance basically determined your fate for love for the rest of your life. If either one of them was terrible, you could count on a miserable future in romance.

I wasn't sure if I was ready to take that chance. But if I was going to be humiliated, I rationed in my brain, I might as well get something significant out of it.

Clarissa watched my facial expressions as she nibbled at her apple core. "You really have nothing to lose." She chewed loudly as she spoke, "He already knows you like him."

Nina leaned in closer to me. "We all know about the picture you took of him yesterday in fifth period."

I wondered how many times I was going to have to be reminded of that. But they were right; he probably already knew I liked him. What did I have to lose? Before I knew it, the contract was back in place, only now the stakes were much higher.

I tossed my empty plate and chocolate milk carton into the garbage and wondered how I'd let that planning session go so horribly. We barely discussed Clarissa asking Jess to dance. I guess it was simpler for her being so mature and all. I walked to fifth period in a daze, almost forgetting that I was about to see Trace. I entered the brown-carpeted classroom just as the bell blazed through the hall. Trace was already at his desk, but I was too humiliated to make eye contact with him. I glanced at the back of his head twice during class, but I thought about him, and the contract and the dance—the *last* dance—all through the math lecture. I had approximately three and a half more days of normalcy. After Friday I would never be able to look at him again.

chapter three

The final bell rang at two fifty, and I walked to the front of the school where Jess was leaning against the outer brick wall, waiting for me. He was wearing the same three-quarter-length baseball shirt that he wore every Thursday.

"It's my Thursday shirt," was always his answer when I teased him about wearing it so often.

The sun was shining on his shaggy, light brown hair, and he looked younger than usual. Maybe it was the red yo-yo he had wrapped around his finger. He held it up to me as I approached. "I won it in geometry for being on time to class every day this semester."

I stuck my tongue out at him. "Goody-goody."

I wanted to tell Jess about the Valentine's dance. Nothing seemed to be real until I had said it out loud to Jess. But if I told him about Trace, then I would have to tell him about Clarissa, and that would ruin everything.

"You're sure quiet today," Jess said as he twirled the yo-yo around his finger. "You okay?" I realized that we had been walking for almost five minutes in silence. I just couldn't think of anything else to say with such a huge issue pressing against my eyeballs. I gave in, like I always did with Jess.

"No, I'm not okay." Jess stopped twirling his yo-yo and looked at me intently as we walked. I looked ahead, but I could sense his concern. "It's this stupid Valentine's dance!" Jess relaxed and started twirling his yo-yo again, but through his eyes it was obvious that he was amused.

I shot a glare in his direction. "It's not funny, Jess! Clarissa and Nina are going to ruin my life!"

Jess's voice was calm like my dad's, "How can they ruin your life at a Valentine's dance?"

"They're going to tell Trace that I like him and ask him if he likes me back! Then they're going to ask him to dance with me—the *last dance!*"

"Wow." Jess raised his eyebrows, but other than that remained emotionless. "Sounds romantic."

"Not romantic." I emphasized the "ck" sound for effect. "Humiliating!"

"Doesn't he already know that you like him?"

I stopped walking and scowled sourly at Jess.

"I mean, you *did* take a picture of him in the middle of class."

He said it so nonchalantly. I was fuming mad. "Jess! I didn't *mean* to take the picture of him! He just *thinks* that I meant to take it of him!"

"Right, and he *thinks* you like him."

"But I don't!"

"Yeah, you do."

"But he doesn't *know* that, and if Clarissa and Nina tell him, then he'll *know!*"

"So why are you letting them do it?"

Oh no, this was the part that I was dreading. "I can't tell you."

"Why can't you tell me?"

"No, shhh!" I held my index finger up to his mouth, and I could feel his lips curve into a smile under my finger. "I can't tell you," I said between gritted teeth, "so don't ask."

We started walking again as Jess tried to make sense of what I was telling him. "Okay, so for some reason that I can't know about, you are allowing Clarissa and Nina to... what were the words you used... ruin your life?"

I sighed deeply and looked down the long, narrow road in front of us. Gigantic evergreens taller than skyscrapers lined the road as far as the eye could see. There were two routes between our street and the school. In the mornings we would always take the faster and more boring route through the S-shaped streets of our neighborhood. But on the way home from school, we would take the adventurous route. It was technically a shortcut, but Jess and I didn't rush the adventurous route. Our junior high was in the middle of town, but Jess and I lived next to Emery Lake. The land between the lake and town center was hidden by endless acres of forest. Lush, green needles that would leave an ever-present dew sparkling between their branches covered the hills like a wet cloth. There was an amazing contrast of their red trunks and rich brown pine cones that seeped deep into my blood. The forest was our playground.

After cutting through the trees on a half-mile long path through the woods, Jess and I would cross over a brown grassy area that was once a community soccer field. The field was overgrown now with weeds and scattered pine branches, but the old soccer stands were still in place, some of them loose and considered a hazard by grown-ups. Jess and I spent most of the afternoon sun hours hanging from the soccer stands or trying to hit them with stray rocks. Today, however, was a serious day containing a severe dilemma, and I walked placidly through the field. "I don't know," I finally responded, "maybe there's just a part of me that wants Trace to know the truth. Maybe it's time I take a chance and see what will happen." I felt liberated with my new-found bravery, and the sun seemed to beat down on me harder than before.

"See what will happen?" Jess smirked. "What can *happen*, Gem? You're fourteen years old."

I hated it when Jess told me my age. I could feel the blood rushing to my face as I balled up my fists at my sides. "Oh! And you're so old and mature!"

"No, I don't think that I'm old and mature, which is the reason that I'm *not* the one fretting over my *love* life."

That only made me angrier. "I'm not *fretting*, Jess!" But I knew that wasn't true, which only made me angrier. "And as for my love life—I think I should have the right to do what I want! I'm not a little girl anymore, Jess! I'm a teenager!" I took a deep breath and stamped my foot. "I even wear a *bra!*" That word, that disgustingly putrid word, escaped from my mouth—much too loudly—like a bullet from a presumably unloaded gun. Jess's eyes widened, and his whole face turned a shade of pink. He immediately averted his eyes away from me and followed the swinging motion of his yo-yo with deep concentration. I couldn't believe I had just said the word *bra* in front of Jess. There were about five words in my vocabulary that I absolutely would not say in front of him, and *bra* was at the top of the list.

The thick silence between Jess and I was nauseating, and I cringed at the thought of how terrible this day had turned out. I grunted quietly as I kicked an empty Coke can toward the fence. Jess stiffly looked toward the can and then down at my foot. He couldn't even look at me in the eyes. I turned my glare toward him without moving my head. My face was molded into a deep scowl in order to outwardly show my contempt toward him and the entire situation. We slowly made eye contact and without any warning at all Jess's eyes began to crinkle as his face lit up.

"What's so funny?" I was still scowling as Jess began to laugh softly. "This day is so stupid," I said with a slight stomp in my foot.

We didn't say another word to each other as we made our way across the final yards of the big field.

On the opposite end was a barbed-wire fence that separated the field from our neighborhood. A small hole was put in the fence, probably years ago by some rebellious teenage boys, and over time the hole had grown to be big enough to crawl through. Jess held up the loose fencing wire for me to crawl through. I made my way through carefully—though I had done it so many times by that point that I could probably do it blindfolded—and waited for Jess to toss me our backpacks before climbing through himself. The other side of the opening introduced a whole new playground. Massive walls of concrete blocks lay in ruins where construction of a small storage unit had started once until the owner went bankrupt, leaving a maze of cinder blocks for Jess and me to play on.

We called it our concrete jungle.

Most of the block walls were low enough for us to see over—though I had to be on my tiptoes. But some walls were high enough that we could climb them and see over the trees and roof tops of the surrounding houses. The lot itself was about the size of a tennis court, but it seemed a lot bigger with the maze of block walls. Jess and I were pretty much the only people who ever went there, though every once in a while we found an old cigarette butt or an empty pop can, indicating that someone else had trespassed there while we were in school or fast asleep.

I tossed both Jess's backpack and my own on a pile of blocks and headed over to the first high wall. I sensed Jess's hesitation to follow me. Lately he had been having these strange ideas that he was too old to climb the blocks. I usually told him to get real and come on. But today I didn't push him.

I pulled a peanut butter granola bar out of my pocket that I had snagged on my way out of my house that morning. I plopped down on the blocks and swung my legs against the wall as I chewed into my snack. This particular wall was probably a good ten feet off the ground, but the blocks were thick, and I wasn't scared of heights. I was two bites into my granola bar when Jess climbed the blocks and sat next to me, swinging his legs to my rhythm—still playing with his yo-yo.

"You want to know a secret?" Jess said, watching his yo-yo go up and down.

"Of *course* I want to know a secret," I replied without hesitation—who didn't want to know a secret?

"Remember last Wednesday when I couldn't walk home with you because I went home with a kid from my class to work on a group project?"

"Yes," I mumbled—that was a miserable thing for him to do.

"Well, we were in the kid's bedroom working on the project—there were about four of us guys—and he pulled up some pictures on his laptop." Jess didn't have to say what kind of pictures they were. I could tell from his posture and the way he bit his lip that they weren't pictures of outer space or famous athletes. I had never actually seen pornography, but I had heard it joked about once on a rerun of *Friends,* and my mom had made me change the channel.

"Did you look at it?" I knew I had no right to ask, but Jess and I asked each other questions that we had no right to ask all the time. Jess was still looking down at his yo-yo, which he was now holding still in his clutched hands.

"No, but the other guys did. I didn't know what to do, so I just kept coloring in maps for our project. It was the worst feeling." Jess ran his fingers through his hair. "I hated it."

"Did they make fun of you?" I kept swinging my legs to act as natural as possible.

"Yeah, sort of, but mostly they were just embarrassed I think. After it was over, when one of the guys' moms picked us up to take us home, it was so weird." I studied Jess's face for a couple seconds and then looked out ahead at the forest of tree. "I'm telling you this," Jess continued, "because I don't want you to think you're alone in this whole weird growing up thing. And I'm sorry I said that nothing could happen with that Trace kid. He probably does like you, and I hope you get to dance with him."

"The last dance," I grumbled.

"Yeah, the last dance." Jess weakly raised one corner of his mouth. "And look how mature you are—we both are—sitting here on this wall having a grown-up conversation and all. It feels nice."

I was still quiet. I hated the idea of growing up.

I hated bras, and I hated dances, and I hated grown-up conversations.

"Do you want a bite of my granola bar?" I asked Jess—trying to change the subject. He grabbed the granola bar from my hand and took a bite off the end.

"The last dance," Jess repeated as he chewed. "I wouldn't dance with a girl on the last dance if someone paid me." I jerked my gaze toward Jess's face and angrily grabbed the granola bar back from his hand.

"Why not?"

Jess shrugged his shoulders. "Because, the last dance is always blown up into being such a huge deal like you're supposed to end up marrying the person or something."

"But what if someone *asks* you to dance the last dance?"

Jess looked at me surprised. "What are you so uppity about?"

I squeezed the granola bar tightly in my hand and felt it change form. "You can't just decide that you're not going to dance, Jess! If someone asks you, you can't say no!"

"What's the big deal?" He was eyeing his yo-yo again as he spoke.

I took the last bite of my granola bar and talked with a full mouth. "I just don't want you to be socially awkward. People see me with you every day, and it would be bad for my reputation."

Jess twisted his mouth. "Trust me, Gem, I think taking pictures of guys in class will do far more damage to your reputation than me not dancing the last dance." Jess laughed and threw his yo-yo across the lot onto a pile of dirt. "I'm terrible at those things. Come on," he pushed himself off the cement wall, "let's get you home."

chapter four

Ten minutes later I opened the door to my house
and took a deep sigh. I knew I was getting older when I started
sighing. I tossed my backpack onto the floor and headed into the
kitchen. My mom was in the same place that I had left her that
morning. She had the same apron on—different clothes underneath it—and the same happy Mom smile to say hello that she
had worn when she said good-bye eight hours before. I was glad
that Mom was home because I needed to tell her about school. I
needed to tell her about all the weird things that had happened
since I left that morning, and I needed her to tell me that everything would work out. I made sure that I made a lot of noise as I
collapsed in the barstool behind her.

She had obviously gotten the hint. "What's the matter, Gemma?"

"Today was the worst," I huffed. Mom kept stirring her sauce
or soup or whatever she was making, but she was looking at me
with a furrowed brow, and I knew I had her attention. I told her

about Nina and Clarissa and their stupid idea, and I told her the other side of it about Clarissa asking Jess to dance.

Mom tapped her big wooden spoon on the edge of the pot and laid it on the counter. She examined the contents of the pot but spoke to me, "I think you should forget about Trace and dance with Jess yourself." She walked to the refrigerator and pulled out a head of lettuce. I moaned when she said it and put my head on the counter in front of me. I gave a similar reaction every time my mom talked about me and Jess in a romantic way. The garage door opened, and I heard my dad's soft footsteps in the side hall. He walked into the kitchen when my mom was midsentence. "I think he will make such a great husband someday."

Dad raised his eyebrows, "Husband?"

"Hi, Dad," I said, making sure my voice still sounded exasperated. Mom spoke in a higher notch as she said, "Hi, honey," and kissed him on the lips. I watched them carefully, trying to figure out how they did it without bumping noses.

"What's all this talk about husbands?" Dad continued as he wiggled out of his coat and flipped off his shoes.

Mom answered, "Oh, Gemma is going to ask a boy to dance this Friday at the Valentine's dance, and she's nervous about it." Is *that* what she got out of it? I've been pouring my heart out to this woman for the past twenty minutes, and *that's* how she rephrased it?

"Mom!" I exclaimed. "He's not just any boy! And it's not just any dance! It's the *last* dance!"

Mom pulled a dish full of baked potatoes out of the oven. "Oh, right," she said, only half paying attention. "Didn't I mention that?"

The garage door opened again, but this time it was Bridget. She had just gotten her driver's license, and she made a huge scene when she came through the garage door, reminding us that she was now a licensed driver. She was barely inside when my dad asked, "Is the car still in one piece?"

"Ha, ha," Bridget answered sarcastically as she tossed her purse on the kitchen table. She flung the car key ring around her index finger a few times before placing it carefully on the key holder. "Dad, you would be amazed at how good of a driver I am. I think I'm ready to drive my friends to Atlanta for spring break." She gave him a hopeful smile waiting for his answer.

Dad snorted through his nose. "Bridget, you might as well not get your hopes up because the first time you drive to Atlanta will be in your own car with your own insurance when you're twenty-five." Bridget moaned, and Dad chuckled into the junk mail that he was hastily scanning.

"Oh, Bridge!" Mom practically whistled as she handed me four placemats. "Don't put those keys away too soon. I need you to take Gemma to her piano lesson as soon as we're done eating." Mom's newfound indulgence of ditching the drive-Gemma-around chore to Bridget was my newfound drudgery. I buried my head into my arms on the counter and whimpered a muffled cry into my hands.

"I hate driving with Bridget! I got so sick the last time I rode in the car with her that I had to roll the window down." Bridget walked past me and smeared her hand down the front of my face. I pulled away from her and scowled as she stole a cucumber out of the salad. Mom was obviously too enthralled with her cooking to be swayed by my pleadings, so I turned to my dad. "Dad! You have to hear me out! Piano lessons are bad enough without feeling nauseous by the time you get there!"

Bridget stuck her tongue out at me.

"Just keep your window rolled down, Gemma. The fresh air will do you good." From my dad, the optimist.

'I walked to the kitchen window and tore open the drapes. "It looks like it's going to snow!" I said infuriatingly. "I'll catch pneumonia!" Dad was still looking at the mail. How he managed to pay attention to our conversations and read his mail at the same time was beyond me. Eventually he looked at Mom, who was grating cheese into the salad. "How did we manage to conceive such a drama queen?"

A drama queen? Maybe I was overreacting a little. I mean, Bridget's driving wasn't *that* bad. But I just couldn't bring myself to be calm about the Valentine's dance. Maybe it was just a stupid dance. And maybe I was being dramatic. But at that moment I simply couldn't imagine life getting any worse.

chapter five

I looked down at my dress as I stood awkwardly outside the doors of my school's gymnasium. The bottom ruffle by my knees was wrinkled from sitting on it all day in classes, and I wasn't sure if my flat red shoes matched the red in my skirt. It seemed a little off. Clarissa and Nina had insisted that they go into the bathroom to look at themselves in the mirror before going into the dance. The noise coming from the girl's bathroom was loud, and I could smell hairspray all the way out in the hall. I wasn't about to go in there. So I stood by myself, gazing nervously through the open doors that led to the big room full of giggling teenagers and blaring music.

The gymnasium, which was the size of one full basketball court, was stripped of all of its athleticism. The main lights were off, and the only lighting came from a pink, blue, and green disco ball at the front of the room near the disk jockey table. Crepe paper and balloons—the same style that had been in the hall all week—hung from the ceiling and doors. In fact, it looked like the ninth-grade activities committee had just stripped the halls of all their decorations and hastily taped them all over the gymnasium. I tried to sigh, but I was too nervous to catch a full breath. I was starting to feel nauseous when Clarissa and Nina appeared at my sides.

"Ready?" Clarissa asked with a bubbly voice. This was just the sort of thing that she had been waiting all year for. It had the opposite effect on me. I couldn't stop thinking about Trace and the last dance. I hadn't seen him yet, and I was glad. Maybe he wasn't here. Maybe he had gotten permission to check out early. A flash of relief and disappointment swept through me.

Clarissa and Nina each took one of my hands as we walked carefully through the opened double doors. I'm sure we looked utterly insecure and dorky. But that's exactly what we were. The room was huge, but it seemed even bigger being crammed with three hundred seventh, eighth, and ninth graders. Most of the ninth graders were crowded up front by the disco ball. I spotted a few kids that I recognized as eighth graders standing in the middle talking, and it was obvious that the seventh graders were the small kids lined up against the surrounding walls. I was about to go take a place beside them when Clarissa started leading our little trio to the front of the room. I anchored my feet to the wood floor.

"Where are you taking us?" I asked between my teeth, my eyes wide with horror.

Clarissa looked at me with disgust. "There is no way we are staying back here with all the lame eighth graders."

"But we *are* lame eighth graders!" I rebutted.

"Gemma!" Clarissa stomped her foot. "You cannot expect to dance the *last* dance with anyone if you don't get out there and show them what you can do!"

"But I can't *do* anything! I don't know how to dance or shimmy or even sway side to side without looking like an idiot!"

Clarissa rolled her eyes and looked at Nina. "This seriously should have come up before today." She looked back at me. "Just do what I do and you'll be fine." She then pulled me harder than I was expecting, and I stumbled forward, towing quiet Nina behind me.

Clarissa led us straight past the scattered eighth graders and into the squashed group of ninth graders at the front of the room. We bumped into a different person every step we took. I could feel their eyes blaring into my skull, and I knew they were wondering why a group of eighth graders—and not even *cool* eighth graders at that—were invading their personal space.

"Who invited the beanie babies?" a loud male voice boomed from somewhere in the crowd. I knew he was referring to us, and so did everyone else who stared at us in silence. I was too afraid to look toward the voice that sounded much too old to belong to a junior high student. I stopped breathing completely. I wanted to turn around and run out the back door and not look behind me until I was safely outside the school boundaries. But then I heard a familiar voice. "Leave them alone, Conrad." I turned around, and so close to me I could hear him breathing was my Jess. I was so happy to see him I could hardly contain myself. But I had to stay cool. Screaming and giving him a big hug like I wanted wouldn't help either one of our reputations. Thankfully, Jess didn't care much about his. He put his hand on my shoulder and squeezed it gently. "Hey."

Conrad let out a loud, mocking, "Ha! Dating an eighth grader, are we, Tyler?" He flashed his white teeth at the crowd forming around us then glared back at Jess. "I would have thought someone like *you* would set your standards a little higher than that."

Jess kept his hand on my shoulder as he turned toward Conrad. He wasn't flustered in the least. "I wouldn't let it bother you, Conrad. I'm sure there will be a girl left for you." He lifted his shoulders. "And then you'll have a whole new set of things to worry about." And with that Jess looked away, as though Conrad was no more than a helpless mouse.

Conrad watched us skeptically before growing bored and turning back into the crowd. I looked at Jess, bewildered. I had never seen him like this. I mean he talked smack to me all the time. But we were just joking around. I didn't know he talked that way to big, burly guys named Conrad. I looked around at the ninth graders standing around us. I couldn't help but notice the way all the girls looked at him with their flirting eyes—willing him to look at them. I looked back at Jess, who was oblivious to their pining.

I was about to speak when Clarissa let go of my hand and shimmied her way between Jess and me, knocking his hand loose from my shoulder.

"Hey, Jess!" Clarissa spoke in an unnaturally high voice. "Thanks for bailing us out. You made that guy look like a total idiot!"

Jess's face turned downward, and he almost looked concerned. He looked back toward the direction that Conrad went. "Conrad's not such a bad guy."

"Well, I don't think *you're* such a bad guy either." Clarissa shifted her hips so that she stood closer to Jess. I watched him carefully as Clarissa shamelessly flirted. He looked confused.

As a slow song started over the speakers, Clarissa reached up and twirled her index finger in Jess's hair. "Do you want to dance?"

My jaw dropped to the floor. What was she *doing?* And *how* was she doing it? I have to say the only person on the dance floor who looked more disorientated than me was Jess. He clearly did not see that coming.

"Uh, well," he cleared his throat and stumbled over a few more words, "sure."

My feet felt like they were cemented to the ground as Jess and Clarissa stepped away from the tightly packed group so they could dance. Jess glanced back at me and pulled a face before they faded into the darker area of the gymnasium. I continued to watch as Clarissa wrapped her arms much too tightly around Jess's neck, and he awkwardly placed his hands on her waist. I hated seeing them together. I hated it when she let her head fall back with laughter at whatever he was saying, and I hated watching him grip her waist tighter when she nearly tripped over his shoe. I couldn't figure out why I was so angry at them. I was the one who wanted them to dance. I was the one who set this whole thing up! And now it was taking everything I had to not pounce on them and tear their hands from each other like a referee in a boxing match.

The song was over before I realized that I had stood in the same position, watching them through the entire song. I quickly shifted my gaze to the disco ball as they made their way back to Nina and me.

A moment later Nina leaned in behind me and whispered in a fluttery sing-song voice, "Trace incoming." The sound of his name made me panic, and my breath caught at the bottom of my throat. I wanted to rewind back to the beginning of the week and tell Clarissa—stupid Clarissa!—that I did *not* want to dance with Trace, and she could *not* ask him if he liked me. That stupid deal! To think that the only thing I was getting out of this was Clarissa asking Jess to dance—the very scene that just made me want to puke!

When Clarissa and Nina stepped away to decide how to approach Trace, I stole a glance at him standing against the far wall. He was wearing a dark blue dress shirt with a silver tie and black slacks. He looked like he'd stepped straight out of a *GQ* magazine. But other than his suit, he looked exactly the same. He didn't need to make a special effort for the dance, I thought; he just always looked dreamy.

Jess must have seen me looking at him. "There's Prince Charming. I was wondering when we were going to get this show on the road."

"I'm glad you're getting a kick out of watching my dignity being flushed down the toilet."

"Just tell Clarissa and Nina that you don't want them to do it. They're your friends. They'll respect that."

I shook my head. "It's too late. We had a deal, and Clarissa has already done her part of the deal."

"What was her part of the deal?" We both looked at Clarissa, who looked as if she didn't have a worry in the world. "I have the feeling that her side of the deal was a bit easier than yours."

I felt sweat building up underneath my armpits. "It was so *easy* for her. She just walked right up and asked you to dance, like it was no big deal."

Jess's eyes widened. "What? You told Clarissa she could do all of this to you if she would just ask *me* to dance?"

I couldn't do anything but nod.

"Wow, if I would have known she was asking out of obligation, I would have said no. She has so much hairspray on that I swear it is sticking to the walls of my lungs." Jess let out a fake cough.

"I'm so sorry," I started. "It was a stupid bet and I shouldn't have gotten you in the middle of it."

Jess's fake coughing turned into a smothered bout of laughter. "You're not mad?"

"Mad?" He stopped laughing. "How could I be mad? You are basically hyperventilating over here because Clarissa and Nina are going to tell Trace you like him, all because you thought you were helping me dance with a girl that you *thought* I liked. How could I be mad at you for that?" Jess cleared a stray eyelash from my cheek. "I don't deserve a friend as good as you."

Jess's closeness eased my nerves, and I felt my breathing slowing down to a more even pace. I almost forgot the whole terrible situation going on around me when Jess looked over my head and said, "Uh-oh."

I twisted around to face what he was looking at. Through the crowd I saw Clarissa and Nina, standing in front of Trace Weston!

No! I yelled in my head, but no word came out of my mouth. I wanted to scream, but it was too late. The damage was being done, and there was nothing that I could do. But I didn't have to watch. Without looking back at Jess, I bolted from the tight group of ninth graders and headed straight for the double doors that led to the hall. Without stopping, I went straight into the bathroom, which was still packed with giddy teenage girls and their disgustingly potent body sprays. I didn't look at anyone as I shimmied my way into the stall farthest away from the door and locked the stall door behind me. How could this be happening to me? How did I let it get this far? I wanted to cry, but I didn't let myself. I wasn't wearing any makeup, so I didn't have to worry about mascara smearing—a problem that I'd *heard* other girls had when they cried—but I couldn't bear to face anyone at my first Valentine's Dance with red, puffy eyes. When enough time had passed that I was sure the illusive conversation between Clarissa,

Nina, and Trace was over, I allowed myself to open the squeaky pink stall door. I was now alone in the bathroom. I guessed that meant the dance was almost over. No one wanted to be in the bathroom for the last dance, just in case someone happened to ask them.

I willed myself to walk out of the bathroom and into the hall one lead footstep at a time. I gradually reentered the gymnasium. It felt smaller this time. Clarissa and Nina were up by the ninth graders again, talking to each other. Jess was by the back wall, drinking punch with a couple other ninth grade boys. I didn't look for Trace. I wouldn't be able to bear making eye contact with him now. As soon as Clarissa and Nina saw me, they ran over to me—both of them looking awkward in their way too grown-up high heels.

"Gemma! We asked him!" Nina balled up her fists like a cheer leader.

"What did you say? What did *he* say?" I braced myself for their answers.

Clarissa spoke this time, "We just told him you liked him!" She shrugged her shoulders as though it wasn't a big deal at all. "He didn't seem that surprised. And then we told him that if he likes you back he should ask you to dance the last dance."

I felt so exposed.

"He smiled!" Nina added, and her words changed the situation entirely.

I looked straight into Nina's eyes, then to Clarissa's. "He smiled? Really? A nice smile or a disgusted smile?"

Clarissa looked at Nina questioningly. "Mmm, hard to say."

"No," Nina disagreed, "it was definitely a nice smile."

"Don't get her hopes up," Clarissa said as though I weren't standing right there.

At that moment the music was hushed and our principal's voice blared through the speakers, "The next song is going to be our last, so let's see everyone out on the dance floor. And be safe on your way home."

A romantic song started as everyone around me began to break off into pairs. Nina and Clarissa were asked to dance before the introduction was over, leaving me standing alone waiting for Trace to find me in the crowd. I could feel my face starting to get hot as the singer began the first verse. I wondered how long the song was, and I wondered how long I should wait for Trace. I had just about given up when I felt a warm hand on my shoulder. I stopped breathing as I slowly turned around. It was Jess.

"Hey," he smiled apologetically, "I know I'm not the person you wanted to see right now, but—"

Before he could finish, I threw my arms around his neck. "I couldn't *be* happier to see you!" I squeezed him so hard. Maybe I was holding on for dear life. I knew that if I let go I would slip into the most humiliating experience of my life.

Jess grimaced when I finally let go of his neck. "No Trace, huh?"

I shook my head.

"Well, I know I said I would never dance the last dance, but I figure—"

"I would *love* to!" I quickly stepped toward Jess, but he stepped away as quickly as I moved in. "What's wrong?" I felt a pang of embarrassment flash through my body. Maybe he hadn't been asking me to dance after all.

"We can't dance right here."

I looked around me. We were in the back of the gymnasium

right by the punch table. The only people around us were teach-ers and a couple of uncomfortable and un-asked seventh graders. "Okay, where should we go then?" I was afraid of his answer. If I knew Jess as well as I thought I did he'd want us to go out on the soccer field away from the rest of the crowd. So I was surprised when he pointed to the front of the room where the ninth graders were packed together. "Up there? There's no room!"

"Sure there is. Besides, we have to let this Trace kid know what he's missing."

Jess took hold of my hand and led me toward the front of the gymnasium. Holding his hand made me feel safe from the disappointment that was surrounding my head. Jess stopped as soon as we were close enough to the crowd to look "involved" but far away enough to breathe. He pulled my hand across my body until I spun under his arm. When I had completed the spin, I was locked safely in his arms.

"Are you kidding me?" I looked up at his face and was sur-prised to see him so close.

He looked genuinely confused. "What?"

"Where did you pull that move from? Mr. 'I wouldn't dance the last dance if someone paid me.' You've always made it sound like you couldn't dance!"

Jess rolled his eyes. "I have two sisters. What do you expect?"

I stared up at Jess; he used to seem so much taller. I didn't realize I had grown so much over the past couple of years. The last time I stood this close to Jess was when he was hoisting me up into our old tree fort in the woods behind my house. That was at least two summers ago. Back then my eye level was about to his chest. Now my forehead came right about to his chin. And he had even grown a couple inches himself. Being this close to him

I couldn't help but take in his smell. Jess wasn't the type to drown himself in cologne, but instead he smelled like fresh soap from this morning's shower mixed with the electrifying scent of men's deodorant. As the song played on, Jess and I stopped talking, and soon we were dancing so close that my cheek was nuzzled into the side of his smooth neck. I always thought that I knew Jess so well. I knew the exact laugh lines that would appear on his face when I made a funny joke. I knew what made him angry, frustrated, or annoyed. I knew when he needed a haircut and when he hadn't studied enough for a test. But in all the years that we had spent together, I had never been this close to him. I had never felt the softness of his skin against my face.

"Can I cut in?"

I knew that piercing female voice all too well.

I pulled myself a few inches away from Jess's firm grasp to see Clarissa standing at our sides with her hands clasped behind her back. Both Jess and I looked at her with our mouths gaping.

Jess spoke first. "Right now isn't a good time," he started. But before he could say more, I interrupted him.

"It's okay, Jess." I was still staring at Clarissa, wondering how she could take Jess away from me now when Trace had obviously decided not to ask me to dance. But I didn't want either one of them to feel sorry for me. I wanted to prove that I was okay on my own. I released my hold on Jess's neck, and I felt him do the same. The air around me felt cold without Jess's heat surrounding me. Jess watched me with uncertain eyes as I stepped away and Clarissa inserted herself in my spot between his arms. I left the dark gymnasium, and even though it was against the rules, I walked down the hall to my locker and took out the bag I had packed with jeans and a sweatshirt. My first last dance had been horrible. Trace didn't like me. And now Jess was dancing with Clarissa for the second time, up close and intimate. I went to a distant bathroom where I could no longer hear the music from the dance. I changed out of my dress and mismatched shoes and put on my comfortable clothes. The clothes that didn't reek of rejection.

chapter six

Twenty minutes later Jess and I were walking across the old soccer field headed for home. So far it was as though the dance had never existed. Jess was playing with a helium balloon when I met him, and he had been sucking out the air and talking like a chipmunk ever since. Once he used up all the helium, he stuffed the saggy balloon in his pants pocket and cleared his throat. "So, Clarissa cut in while we were dancing."

I raised an eyebrow at his subtle approach of bringing the subject up. "Yeah, I know. I was there."

Jess looked down at his shoes as he walked. "You don't *have* to let someone cut in when they ask, you know. It's not a rule."

"Well apparently it's also not a rule to ask someone to dance just because their friends asked you to do it." I kicked at an old wrapper that was floating around on the grass.

"Trace just doesn't know what he's missing."

I knew Jess was just being nice. Trace knew *exactly* what he was missing. He was missing an eighth grade moron who stalked him during algebra class. But it felt better to agree with Jess, so I puffed out my chest and said, "Yeah! Trace Weston doesn't deserve me. I'm done with him!"

Jess clapped his hands once, but then both of our hands fell to our sides. We walked in silence for a moment, soaking up the fact that I had been undeniably rejected today.

I squinted into the sun that was finally peering through the clouds. "Can I ask you a question?"

Jess shrugged his shoulders once. "Sure."

"Are you popular?" I hadn't been able to lose the image of the girls at the dance, how they had watched him and hung on his every movement. Even the guys were impressed by him.

"What are you talking about?" Jess's voice became higher suddenly, like he was embarrassed. He knew exactly what I was talking about.

"Are—you—popular?"

"Gemma, you need to forget that word—*popular*. It doesn't mean anything. It doesn't even exist."

"I knew it." I folded my arms roughly around my chest and scowled at the ground in front of me. "You *are* popular. You're just trying to deny it."

"Where is this coming from?"

"The way you talked to that Conrad guy at the dance and the way all the girls—even the pretty ones—were swooning over you! It's so obvious! I can't believe I never saw it before!"

His hands smacked against the sides of his legs with exasperation. "Popularity doesn't mean anything."

"It *means* that you're cooler than everyone else."

"Says who?"

"Says the other cool people," I fought back.

"What makes them so cool?"

"Nicer clothes, good looks, lots of money." I could have gone on.

"Look at me, Gemma. Do I wear nice clothes?" I looked at his un-tucked blue button shirt that he had on at the dance. His brown tie was now tied around his head like a bandana. Before I could answer, Jess continued, "The reason a lot of people know me and talk to me is because I talk to *them*. It's not about nicer clothes or money or looks."

"No one wants me to talk to them. Everyone thinks they're *so cool*."

Jess sighed. "Nobody in junior high thinks they're cool."

"Humph." I twisted some hair between my fingers. "I don't care anyway. I don't need any of them."

Jess squinted at me. "Sounds like you have it all figured out."

We were approaching the hole in the fence, so Jess reached for my backpack while I climbed clumsily through the hole. When Jess made it through, he stood right in front of me and watched me with serious eyes.

"We've sort of been having some serious conversations lately, haven't we?" His eyes traced the lines of my face as he spoke.

I nodded, but I was physically unable to do anything else. The way he looked at me so closely, putting the rest of the world out of focus, took my breath away, and I couldn't find my voice to speak.

Jess hesitantly lifted his hand toward my face and cleared a stray piece of hair that had blown against my cheek.

My heart was pounding in my throat as I memorized the feel of his skin against mine. His eyes were locked with mine as he tucked the hair behind my ear. But as he lowered his hand, his eyes brightened with a new thought and he stepped around me while saying, "It was kind of sad when Clarissa cut in like that."

I recomposed myself and turned to follow him. "Sad? Why?"

He cocked his head to one side. "Clarissa and that hairspray." He forced himself to cough. "I wonder if it could cause damage to my lungs."

"Plus, you were probably sad that you weren't dancing with me anymore, right?" I was dying to know, but I laced my words with a hint of humor in case the answer wasn't what I wanted to hear.

Jess pursed his lips and nodded with a reciprocating hint of sarcasm. "Really sad."

"I bet it was my mismatched reds that made you miss me so bad. Guys really go for that kind of thing." I resorted to joking because I was nervous—no, terrified—that he actually wasn't sad to have had our dance cut short at all.

Jess let his head fall back. "Yes," he agreed with his lips lifted into a half smile. "Mismatched clothes are irresistible." We were approaching our houses. I hoped that Jess would follow me onto my lawn, but he began heading in the direction of his driveway.

"You shouldn't feel too bad," I spoke louder as Jess continued to widen the gap between us. "I did give you half a dance."

Jess swung around and continued walking backwards as he nearly yelled at me across the street, "Yeah, and maybe one of these days I'll ask you to dance for a reason besides feeling sorry for you."

I knew he was joking—or rather I hoped he was joking—but his words stung, and my shoulders fell with disappointment.

Jess smiled at my response and waved his arm in my direction as he stepped up onto the curb and walked across his lawn. "I'm only joking, Gem."

He turned back toward his house to watch his footing on the porch steps, and as he did he said something that I couldn't quite make out. Because what he said wasn't meant to be heard. What he said almost sounded like—for a moment I thought I heard—he couldn't have possibly said it—but I thought I heard the words, "I asked you to dance because I love you."

chapter seven

Before I could blink it was nearly June, and the energy level throughout the school was rising. Teachers were collecting the last of the make-up homework. Students were cleaning out their lockers, and orange cones were spontaneously showing up around the courtyard awaiting the big summer project of expanding the faculty parking lot. I usually lived for these last days of school. I loved how the hallways always smelled like cleaning liquid from students wiping down the desks and chairs. I loved the scattered boxes in all of the rooms being filled back up with used textbooks and rented calculators. I even loved the cafeteria running out of food because the lunch ladies didn't want to buy more food just to have leftovers after the last days of school. But this year these things made me feel a twinge of sadness. This year wasn't just the end of a school year; it was the end of Jess and me walking to and from school together—again.

I had already encountered this heartbreak once before when he'd gone to junior high without me three years before. Though when I was only eleven, the fact that Jess and I weren't walking to elementary together didn't occur to me until I was getting ready to leave for school the first day of sixth grade. I had been eating my breakfast when I looked at the clock and realized that Jess was late (and he was never late). I slurped down my cereal and hurried to put my shoes on as I casually mentioned to my parents that I was going to go to Jess's house and make sure everything was okay. I remember Mom and Dad looking at each other with concern in their eyes. Dad looked so casual when he told me, "Jess isn't going to be walking you to school this year." He had said it so nonchalantly, as though it was no big deal. Now, I think he knew how big of a deal it really was; he just didn't know how else to say it. My parents had watched me with pained eyes as I melted to the floor, tears streaming down my face. Mom had called the school nurse and told her that I was going to be late for school that morning. I think she felt guilty for not warning me about it earlier. The next nine months of sixth grade had been a lonely time for me, and I was not excited to relive those years again.

But when the final bell rang on my last day as an eighth grader, I was so excited to get out of the dark, dingy school and into the sunshine that I nearly forgot about the tragedy that I was facing. Hoots and hollers rang through the halls as excited kids ran out of the classrooms and into the warm air. Summer vacation had begun. But I was reminded of the sadness when I saw Jess, leaning against the brick school wall with a thick manila folder in hand.

"What's that?" I said when I got close to him.

Jess looked down at the folder. "It's just a bunch of test scores and special projects that I've done over the past three years. I guess they save them for us and give it all back when we graduate from junior high."

"Don't remind me," I said.

"What's the matter, Gem? You're supposed to be happy on a day like this. You're free from school for a full three months."

I shrugged and quietly headed toward the main wooded road while he fell in line beside me. The sun was beating down on our heads. It was the hottest day of the year so far, and the smell of the hot pine made it feel so much more like summer. I couldn't bear to think that this was the last time Jess and I would be walking home together from this school. It would be the last time we'd run through the soccer field and throw rocks at the old goal posts. It would be the last time we'd crawl through the fence into the cement jungle. We stepped silently onto the soccer field when Jess turned to me and said, "Seriously, what's the matter?"

I stared at him with narrow eyes. "You don't *know?*" It made me angry that I was the only one realizing how horrible our separation was going to be. "Next year you're going to high school, and I'm still going to be here in this lame school, and I'm going to have to walk here *alone.* This is the last time we're going to walk to school together, probably *ever!* Next year you'll be driving your own car to school and you'll probably have a girlfriend."

Jess ducked his head and puffed out his bottom lip, but his eyes were smiling. "I tried failing my classes so I could be held back. But I'm just too smart." I didn't think it was funny. When I didn't laugh, Jess lightly punched me in the shoulder with his fist. "Hey. It's not like we're not going to see each other. I live right across the street. I'll be in your face all the time."

I was honestly surprised to hear that. "Really?"

"You'll be sick of me," Jess promised.

With that Jess leaped toward a nearby goal post, swinging from it like a monkey, then he pushed himself forward onto the grass. "Let's go check out our old fort!" he yelled. He was a good twenty yards away from me by then. "We haven't looked at it forever! I wonder if it's still there!" His last words trailed behind him as he started running to the far side of the field. I held tightly to my backpack straps—and his promise—and sprinted after him.

The summer break seemed much shorter than three months. I was finally getting old enough to realize that the "three-month" break that everyone talked about was not really three months at all. By the time school got out, it was practically mid-June, and it started up again in the latter part of August. That was barely more than two months! I figured it was just another way the adult population was trying to fool us kids.

I looked at the cell phone that my parents had given me as an early birthday present and saw that it was already eight fifty-seven p.m. It was the last night of summer. School started the next day, and Jess and I had gone out for one last walk to the snow cone shack. We were approaching our houses as he was telling me his class schedule. He must have noticed me look at my phone because he asked, "What time do you need to be home tonight?"

I glanced at my house and replied, "Nine." Sometimes my mom watched for me out the front window. But the windows were empty, so maybe I could stay a couple minutes longer.

He dropped his shoulders and slipped both hands into his pockets. "We're still going to see each other, Gem. Every day."

I looked down at the cracking sidewalk and shrugged. "I guess." I was terrified that high school would change him. That he would get busy with homework and sports and stop coming over to my house at night. That he would find new friends—or a girlfriend—and forget all about me.

Jess blew a raspberry through his lips and lightly ruffled my hair. "Don't get all melodramatic on me, Gemmalynn Judith." When I acted dramatic, he called me by my full name, which he was convinced would be my "stage" name someday. "You're going to get sick of me. I swear you are."

I bit the inside of my cheek and nodded in agreement, hoping with everything inside of me that he would really be around so much.

I looked at my house again. I was sure it was past nine. I had to go, but leaving meant it was the end of summer. Tears began building up in the corners of my eyes. I tried to stop, but the harder I tried the more they came. Soon the tears were streaming down my cheeks so fast that I swear I could hear puddles forming on the cement sidewalk beneath me.

Jess, clearly stunned with the reaction, pulled me into a hug.

Between sobs I said into his chest, "I hate this."

Jess breathed quietly into my hair and squeezed me even tighter. "You're going to be just fine. I'm the one who should be crying here. I'm going to be a dorky sophomore in a high school with all those older kids driving their fancy cars."

I let myself let go of the tight hold I had on Jess's torso. He was wearing his blue Cubs T-shirt, which he only wore during the summer. It smelled like dirt and pine and the lake. It smelled like summer. I sniffed and backed away from the hug while wiping at my eyes. "Not to mention the fact that your best friend is an even dorkier ninth-grade girl."

Jess bent his head forward and cleared my soaked strands of hair away from my red cheeks. "Well, *that* I'm sort of proud of."

"Gemma!" The voice startled me as I turned toward my house to see Mom standing on the porch, watering a potted plant. She was looking closely at the leaves of the plant, but the way she said my name meant business. I looked back at Jess and grimaced through my tearstained eyelashes. "That's my cue."

Mom continued talking, though her voice was muffled as she dug deep into the plant to pull out a weed. "Thanks for walking Gemma home, Jessie."

"No problem, Mrs. Mitchell."

She finally looked up from the plant. "You start high school tomorrow, don't you?" She set the water pot down on the porch swing. "Gem, you can start making your way inside while Jess and I finish our conversation."

I smirked at Jess and then dragged my feet across my front lawn. Jess kicked at a leaf on the grass. "Yep, I just hope I don't fall for the elevator pass trick."

Mom laughed loudly at Jess's joke. She wrested her knuckles on her hips and looked up at the sky as if looking at a memory. "Do they still sell elevator passes these days?"

Jess looked up at the sky. "I guess I'll let you know after tomorrow."

"Well good luck, and tell your mom I'll call her tomorrow."

"Will do, Mrs. M. Goodnight." Jess's voice faded into the night as Mom followed me through the screen door.

"I sure like him," she said as she locked the door behind us. "And I wouldn't mind if he was my son-in-law someday."

A year ago I would have stuck my tongue out at my mom's hints toward me and Jess having a romantic relationship. But things were different now. *We* were different now. Jess was sixteen. I was almost fifteen. Jess wasn't just the kid across the street anymore. He was someone special–someone who made me feel things that I wanted to keep on feeling.

I sauntered gloomily into our front room, leaving the lights off, and sat down in front of the window. I watched Jess walk over his grass toward his front door with his hands in his pockets again and his head looking down at his shoes. I thought about the hug that we had just shared. How comfortable it had felt to have his arms around me and to be pressed up against his warm, firm chest. I thought about what Jess had said, how he would be around so much that I'd get sick of him. I squeezed my eyes shut for a moment and prayed that it was true. But as Jess opened his front door and slipped out of my sight, I couldn't help but feel that this night was the end of something.

chapter eight

My alarm clock went off at six thirty a.m. I hit the snooze button and rolled over into my pillows. But I didn't fall asleep again like I usually did. The hard reality of Jess starting high school without me sent a pain through my body. I decided that I was too sick to go to school. Maybe Mom would call the school nurse again and tell her that I was going to be late. I lay in bed motionless until my alarm flipped back on again. An old country western song that I had never heard before was playing—which only hindered my progress of rolling out of bed. I heard Mom flip on the hall light and knew that as soon as she realized I was still in bed, she would be knocking on my door.

"Gem?" She tapped her first two knuckles against my door as I had expected. I moaned. "Are you okay?" She peeked her head into my room.

"I don't think I can go to school today," I murmured, taking advantage of my groggy morning voice. "I'm too sick."

Mom stepped gracefully around the door and sat down on the edge of my bed. She put the back of her hand to my forehead. "Hmmm." She furrowed her brow while closely examining my face in the dim light shining in from my window. "Oh yeah, I know what the problem is."

"You do?" I asked, puzzled. Did I actually have a fever?

"Yep. It looks like you have Missing-Jess-itis." She tugged on each of my ears. "It's very common this time of year. Found most commonly in girls named Gemma who have to walk to school *alone*."

I sneered at my mom then pulled my comforter up over my head. My words were muffled as I spoke, "I'm really sick, Mom! I need you to call the school nurse and tell her I'm not going to be able to go to school this year."

Mom breathed a tired laugh as she stood up and yanked my warm blankets off me. "Come on, kiddo. I'll drive you to school today."

She dropped me off in front of the school, and I dragged myself toward the front doors. When I entered the school, there were still a few students hustling through the halls, peering at their class schedules. I flipped my bag around to find my own class schedule, but I couldn't find it anywhere. Panic swept through my entire body, and I prayed silently that I would wake up from this nightmare. I wished that I had looked more carefully at my schedule. I was so concerned with Jess leaving me that I hadn't taken the time to memorize it. I tore my backpack off my shoulder and rummaged through it with the hope that I might be wrong. Being the first day of school, my backpack was basically empty except for one binder with blank paper, a calculator, and a couple of pencils. It didn't take me long to realize that my schedule was still sitting on my desk in my room a half a mile away. I ran back to the main doors and peered through the clear glass, searching for Mom's car. She was long gone. I squeezed my eyes shut, and I tried to bring back the words that I had read a week before when I received my schedule. My mind was blank. I was desperate. I walked as smoothly as I could down the hall until I came to a class with familiar faces. I entered the already open door naturally and sat down in an empty chair on the back row. Luckily the teacher was still talking with a couple students at the front of the class and hadn't noticed me come in. I looked around the class for Nina or Clarissa. Neither one of them was there. One person was there, however, and he was the one person that I wanted to see least of all. Trace Weston was sitting in the second row, but he hadn't turned his head when I came in the room.

"Good morning, class, and welcome to your first day of ninth grade." The teacher was a younger-looking woman with long red hair and rosy cheeks. She was thin and beautiful, and when she smiled her pink grapefruit lips spread across her entire face. "I have such fond memories of my ninth-grade year," she continued while looking each of us directly in the eye. "And I hope you and I will do everything we can to make it just as wonderful for you."

She introduced herself as Miss Campbell and started taking roll. I held my breath when she got to the *K*s. *Please say my name. Please say my name.*

"Michael Karen?"

"Here."

"Brian Jennings."

"Here."

"Samantha Mullen."

"Here."

Mullen? Mullen came *after* Mitchell alphabetically. My stomach sunk. This was the wrong class. Miss Campbell finished the roll and then asked if there was anyone she hadn't called. I opted not to raise my hand. The announcements and the lunch call came on shortly after. I raised my hand for pepperoni pizza. Miss Campbell then instructed us all to get into a big circle so that she could see everybody's faces better. She brought out a big red, yellow, and white beach ball—that she had already blown up—and threw it to one of the boys across the circle from her.

"Whoever is holding the beach ball is the only person who can talk," Miss Campbell explained. "When you are holding the beach ball, tell us your name and then tell us two things about yourself that are true and one thing that isn't true. As soon as you are done, you place the ball in the middle of the circle, and we silently vote on which was the untruth and which were the truths."

I could tell that Miss Campbell was transferred here from an elementary school. This activity resembled something we would have done in the fourth grade. But I think the whole class agreed that it was much better than the alternative—which was work—so we all happily participated. When the ball finally came to me, I squeezed the ball nervously as I spoke.

"When I was seven, I was almost bitten by a rattle snake. Second, I had to get my tonsils out two days before Christmas. And third—"

"Oh, wait!" Miss Campbell interrupted me. As nice as she was, I thought it was rather rude of her to talk when she didn't have the beach ball. I looked at her as I paused midsentence. "You didn't tell us your name. I'm trying to learn everybody's name so I need to hear it as much as possible."

"I thought you weren't supposed to talk without the beach ball," I said in a matter-of-fact tone. The whole class snickered as Ms. Campbell's perfectly gentle face changed to an expression of shock and then irritation.

"I am the *teacher;* the rules don't apply to me." Her jaw was stiff, and her pursed lips turned a shade of white.

"That doesn't seem very fair," I kept going, not because I was a belligerent person, but because I hoped maybe if she got mad enough she would forget to look my name up on the attendance sheet.

It didn't work. "Give me your name, young lady." Her voice was low, and she spoke slowly.

I was about to reveal my secret when the most evil person in the whole world—Jake Jonathan—spoke up before I had the chance.

"Her name is Gemmalynn Judith Mitchell." It was hard to believe that a person so distant, so horrible, so mocking could know something so personal about me as my full name. "And she has a crush on Trace Weston."

I couldn't believe my ears! The whole class erupted in laughter while I waited to wake up from this horrific dream. I stole a quick glance at Trace, who was looking down at his lap. I turned to Ms. Campbell for any retribution, but even she had a slight upward curve in her lips.

I looked back at Jake, who was hunched over laughing, and yelled the only line of defense I could come up with, "You're not supposed to talk! You don't have the ball!"

"Quiet, everyone." Ms. Campbell finally ordered—fifteen seconds too late. As the laughter died down, Ms. Campbell looked back at me. She must have felt some amount of pity toward me because she spoke in a softer, gentler tone.

"Was your name on the roll? I don't remember ... " She picked up the folder that was sitting on her lap then skimmed her finger along a piece of paper that I assumed was the roll. All I could do was wait for Miss Campbell to realize that I wasn't really in her class. She kept rubbing her finger over the middle of the page—I assumed the *M* section—over and over until I was sure she had smudged the ink. "I don't see your name here Gemmalynn." I cringed at my full name and swallowed hard.

"I—I thought I was in this class, but I guess I'm not." Smooth, real smooth. It didn't matter, though; it couldn't get much worse than this.

"Why didn't you raise your hand when I asked if I missed anybody?"

"Uh. Well." I didn't have an answer for her. My lips continued to frantically move up and down.

"I see." Miss Campbell raised her eyebrows. She looked at me as though I was a homeless person trying to sneak into a wedding to steal food. Then another hint of pity swept across her face. "Maybe the roll is wrong. Let's take a look at your class schedule."

Ugh! Not the class schedule! I wanted to freeze time and beg Miss Campbell to just shut up, please! Couldn't we discuss this *after* class instead of right here in front of everyone?

"Could you go get it for me so I can look at it?" she urged. The rest of the class started getting antsy.

"Um, it's in my locker," I lied. I justified that it was my one untruth that Miss Campbell had so rudely interrupted. "I'll look at it later. I probably just read it wrong." A few more kids laughed until Miss Campbell shushed them. She obviously didn't think it was funny anymore.

"You really should keep your schedule on you, but I guess you'll just have to look at it closer and let me know tomorrow." She cleared her throat again and asked a few more kids to please be considerate of others—which I found ironic. "Okay, let's get on with the game then. Gemma, if you'll pass the ball on to the next person." I looked at her in shock. She wasn't even going to let me finish my turn? I wanted to stand up and protest. I had every right to continue playing the game! But then I wasn't sure if that was true. I sheepishly handed the ball to my left without saying a word.

The bell rang ten minutes later, and I quietly gathered up my backpack. As I was leaving the class, I heard a familiar male voice snickering, "Hey, Gemma, here's an untruth—Gemma's *not* a loser!" Of course it was Jake. He and a few other boys hissed some bad words through their teeth, but I didn't turn around. I walked out of the classroom with their sneers stinging the backs of my ears. I walked through the halls toward my locker until I realized I was going to my old locker in the eighth grade hall. This year's locker number would be printed in bold, black ink at the bottom of my class schedule that was still sitting on my desk at home. I didn't know where to go. I couldn't bear to face the embarrassment of going to another wrong class. I walked aimlessly through the foreign ninth grade hall, looking for Clarissa and Nina, but I couldn't see them anywhere. Four minutes later the bell for second period rang, and I was left standing alone. The school had never seemed so huge and unfamiliar. I escaped out a side door before anyone noticed me and found myself on the side of the school where nobody ever goes, near the dumpster. I leaned against the red brick wall and slid my back down it until I was sitting on the gravel pavement. I hugged my knees and tried to think hard about how I was going to survive this day. I thought about running home to get my schedule, but my mom was sure to be there—I couldn't let her see me out of class. I thought about running to the high school to find Jess—he would know what to do—but my day had been humiliating enough without running through a hall full of high schoolers looking for Jess. I came to the conclusion that I had no choice but to sit against the brick wall by the smelly dumpster all day—or at least until lunch.

The sun was hot as it beat down on my scalp, and the tears that I had eventually cried left a sticky white film on my cheeks. I wiped at my eyes and squinted through the sunlight to look at my watch. It was almost eleven thirty a.m. I had sat against the wall for over two and a half hours. Lunch would be starting in five minutes. I hoisted myself off the pavement. My muscles were sore from sitting in one position for so long. I swatted at my pants as small little pebbles that had stuck to them fell to the ground. I was starving and could practically taste the pepperoni pizza in my mouth. I walked to the door and grasped the handle. As soon as I tugged on the door, I realized to my detriment that it was locked. Of course it was. All of the doors—except for the front doors *right* by the principal's office—were always locked from the outside. I sighed and bent my head back to scowl at the sky. Could this day get any worse? I slithered back down into my seat against the brick wall. The pavement was still cool from me shading it from the sun all morning long. I squeezed my knees tight toward my chest and buried my head between them and my body and tried to imagine what it would feel like to be eating my pepperoni pizza.

I heard the final bell ring and hundreds of kids running toward their buses and carpools. When the sounds wound down,

I felt safe to climb the fence behind the dumpster and walk slowly to the front of the school. I watched my surroundings carefully, making sure that no teachers or parents saw me coming around the back corner of the school. When I could see that it was clear, I walked casually in front of the school, down the main road lead-ing from town, over the wooded path, across the old soccer field, through the hole in the fence, passed the cement walls, and down the street to my house. I was about fifty yards from my front door when I noticed Jess sitting on the front step. I felt the familiar salt building up behind my eyes, but I willed the tears away.

"Hey, Jess," I spoke as though I had expected him to be there.

He looked up suddenly from the textbook he was reading on his lap. "Hey! There's the new ninth grader! You look older," he teased. "How was the first day?"

When I reached my yard, I dropped my still practically empty backpack on the grass and melted onto the ground next to it. I laid out flat—as though I was going to do a snow angel on the lawn, closed my eyes, and moaned at the sky.

Jess grimaced. "That good, huh?"

Words came out of my mouth, but I was barely moving my lips. "You don't want to know."

"Okay." Jess shrugged. "You want to hear about my day?"

I nodded awkwardly as the back of my head dug deeper into the grass.

"I only have five classes now, instead of seven. They're longer, though. But I think I'll like my chemistry teacher."

I rolled over to my side so I could look at him while he was talking. I envied his attitude toward school. It wasn't a punish-ment to Jess. It was an opportunity.

"I have two elective classes and three that are required." He stopped and looked at me lying on the ground. "Man, something must really be wrong for you to let me go on this long. What happened today?"

"You wouldn't believe me if I told you," I mumbled into the arm that I was supporting my head on.

Jess got up from the porch step and crawled over to where I was lying on the grass. "What happened?"

I rolled back on to my back and closed my eyes. "Think of the worst possible first day of school that you can think of."

Jess rubbed his face with one of his hands. "I could be here all day."

"Seriously, Jess, haven't you had one of those nightmares where you show up on your first day in just your underwear, and you don't know anyone, and you don't know where you're supposed to go, and everyone is laughing at you?"

"You went to school in your underwear?"

"Take out the underwear part and you have my first day of ninth grade."

Jess situated himself on the grass next to me. "From the beginning."

"I was late getting to school because I was trying to talk my mom into letting me stay home."

"I hate it when that happens." He was teasing me again. I could always tell by the sound of his voice.

"Then when I got there I realized that I had forgotten my schedule."

Jess groaned and covered his eyes with his hands. "That *does* stink."

"So I just went into one of the classrooms."

"You just guessed?"

I nodded and continued, "But the teacher didn't call my name on the roll."

"It was the wrong class." He stated it as though he had just figured out another clue to a puzzle.

I nodded again. "So the teacher has us get in a circle to play this game with a ball, and you could only talk if you had the ball."

"You just stayed in the class anyway?"

"Jess!" I snapped at him for interrupting me and gave him a glare that made him snap his lips together. I continued, "When it was my turn with the ball, the teacher asked my name."

"She shouldn't have been talking! She didn't have the ball!" Jess pointed his finger in the air like he was a lawyer in court.

I was so happy that Jess felt the same way I did. "That's what I said!"

"You *said* that?"

I bit my bottom lip and nodded my head slowly.

"Oh, no." Jess closed his eyes and waited for me to continue.

"So Jake Jonathan told her my name. And while he was at it, he told her and the rest of the class that I like Trace Weston."

"Of all the classes in the whole school, you picked the one with Jake Jonathan?"

"*And* Trace Weston!"

I thought Jess's eyes would bug out of his face. "Trace was in the class, too?"

I looked up at the sky. There was no need to respond.

Jess urged me on, "Then what happened?"

"The teacher figured out that I wasn't supposed to be in the class. She just kept going on and on about it in front of everyone. It was humiliating."

Jess groaned. He genuinely sounded like he was aching inside. "That is rough, Gem. I hope things looked up after that."

"Ha!" I blurted sarcastically. "Not exactly. My whole day's schedule was here in my bedroom!" I pointed at my house. "Even my locker number was on the stupid piece of paper! I couldn't do anything."

Jess narrowed his eyes. "So what did you do?"

"I sat outside by the dumpster until everyone had gone home."

Jess pitched his head forward. "All day?"

"Yes," I said matter-of-factly. "What else was I supposed to do?"

"Gemma, you could have just gone to the office. They have copies of everyone's schedules. They would have just printed you off a new one!"

Jess's obvious answer hurt my ears. I felt so stupid and embarrassed and mad. Tears welled up in my eyes with full force. There was no willing them away this time. "Well that's just great!" I blubbered as I hit the grass in front of me. Jess's expression immediately changed from surprised to apologetic. He wrapped his arm around me and pulled me into his chest.

"I'm sorry, Gemma. I shouldn't have said it like that. I probably wouldn't have known that either. The only reason I do is because my teacher in seventh grade spilled her coffee on my schedule and she told me to go to the office to get a new one. There's no reason you would have known that."

I wiped at my eyes and sat straight again. "So anyway," I sniffed and dabbed at my nose, "that was my first day of ninth grade." I was still trying to clean up my face when the front door of my house swung wide open.

"Gemmalynn Judith!" Mom spoke sternly. There was serious anger in her eyes. "Could you explain to me why your principal just called to inform me that you weren't at school today?" Mom was one of the most genuinely nice people I knew, but you did not want to get on her bad side. She had an aura about her that demanded respect.

Jess got up from the lawn and picked his book up off the porch step. "Uh, I better get home to do some homework." Jess knew as well as anybody—regardless of the fact that Mom liked him better than anybody—that it wasn't in his best interest to be around when she was angry. I begged him with my eyes to stay. I knew that the reprimand would be less severe if he was around. He glanced at me with apologetic eyes. "See you later, Gem." Then with his head turned away from Mom, he mouthed, "Good luck." And he took off across the street.

"Gemma!" Mom's razor-sharp voice sliced through the silence. "I'm waiting for an explanation." How a woman so petite could be so terrifying is something I'm still trying to figure out.

I looked up at her, my face still stained with tears.

"And don't think that any amount of crying is going to get you out of trouble, young lady!"

I tried to speak, but my throat caught as more tears spilled out of my eyes. My mom's anger immediately turned into concern. "Are you all right, Gemma? Did something happen?" She double stepped the porch stairs and kneeled at my side.

Oh, no. Now she was worried that something really bad happened. She'd only be more upset when she found out that physically I was just fine (though I couldn't say the same about myself mentally or emotionally). I sniffed hard and shook my head. "No, I'm okay. I just had a really bad day, that's all."

She folded her arms and bent her head toward me,"I'm waiting, *impatiently,* to hear your side of the story."

I told her everything—starting with the moment I realized I didn't have my schedule and ending with me spending the day next to the dumpster.

Her first response was, "Why didn't you just go to the office?" But when I started to cry again, she backed off slightly. "You didn't know that you could get a copy there?"

I buried my head in my hands and shook my head. She rubbed the back of my head then pulled me close to her with her hand. "That does sound like a rough day." She even chuckled slightly as she let what I told her run through her brain.

Mom picked herself up off the grass. "Okay." She took my hand and hoisted me to my feet. "I'm not mad at you, Gem. But I'm disappointed that you decided to sit outside all day long rather than let me or another adult know you had a problem. So to help you remember that in the future, you're going to be weeding my garden every day after school for the rest of the week. Got it?"

"Ah! Weeding!" That was worse than sitting by the dumpster!

The next day my mom drove me to school again so she and I could explain to the principal what happened. I then went to all of my assigned classes, having to explain to each and every single teacher what had happened. The only thing worse that my first day of ninth grade was having to retell it eight times the next day. I barely saw Clarissa or Nina the whole day. Clarissa wasn't in any of my classes, but I saw her from a distance, standing at her locker. And even though I had World History with Nina, she sat on the other side of the room with a couple other girls she'd met over the summer at dance camp. I went from class to class sitting in the back rows—since the closer desks had all been claimed by students the day before—silently scribbling on the blank paper in my binder, and occasionally taking notes when the teacher specifically told us we should write something down. I went through the lunch line alone and sat at the end of one of the long lunch tables until I was instructed by a group of boys that I was sitting in *their* seats. I took the rest of my lunch to the library and ate at one of the tables in the back until the librarian told me I couldn't have food in the library. And worst of all, because my family was, yet again, in Cape Cod during regular registration, my locker was in the "late registration zone"—in the eighth grade hall! What was happening? I thought I was supposed to automatically be cool in ninth grade. I was part of the oldest grade in the school! I was a *freshman!* So why did I feel like a dorky seventh grader all over again? It occurred to me in my seventh-period geography class that I hadn't spoken to anyone all day—besides the principal and my teachers, to explain my absence the day before. I sat in my chair in the back, only partly listening to Mr. Haggard reciting a poem about the continents, when I had another realization. Clarissa, Nina, and Jess were the only friends I had. If they weren't around, I had no one else to talk to! Sure, I would have an occasional conversation here or there with a girl I had known since elementary. But the only *real* friends—the people who noticed when I was absent—were Clarissa, Nina, and Jess. And I doubt that the first two even noticed that I was gone yesterday. The strange thing was that I wasn't even distraught in the least about Clarissa and Nina. Their friendship had only made my life harder. But what shocked me was that I was this old and I had so few friends. I wasn't so unattractive that people couldn't bear to look at me. I was fun to be around and had a good sense of humor, at least Jess thought so. So, why was it so impossible for me to make another friend?

That night before bed I pulled out an old notebook and began listing the people in school that I could potentially be friends with. By the time I came up with four names, I had already crossed each of them out for various reasons. Too weird. Bad breath. Squeaky voice. One too many body piercings. Maybe I was meant to go through my ninth grade year alone. I had just come to this conclusion when I heard the familiar sound of tiny rocks hitting my window.

I walked over to my window and lifted up the old wooden frame. I looked down, and fifteen feet below was Jess's moppy brown hair bouncing around while he looked for more small pebbles to throw at my window.

I spoke in a normal voice, "Hey!"

Jess's face suddenly appeared beneath his tousled hair as he stared up the side of the house toward my window. His pensive expression broke into a smile of relief.

"Hey," he spoke in a lower voice, even though I had told him a million times that no one could hear us. "You're awake."

I cocked my head to the side. "As if a little thing like me sleeping would really stop you."

Jess motioned for me to come down. I shook my head at him. "It's too early. My dad hasn't gone to bed yet. He's downstairs watching TV." I lowered my voice to the same volume as Jess's. "Things are going sour a bit early tonight, aren't they?"

The top of Jess's head appeared again as he lowered his face and looked at the ground.

I sat watching him, not understanding the depth of what he lived with day in and day out, but knowing that he was in pain. And for some reason, he always picked my window to come to as an escape. "Stay there," I said. "I'll be right down."

Jess's head shot up again, and I saw the pleading in his eyes that what I said was true. It always threw me off a little to see such vulnerability from him when he stood underneath my window—a side of him that he hid from everyone, even me—during the daylight hours.

"But what about your dad?"

"I'll just tell him that you need me."

"There's no way he'll let you out." Jess would never say it, but I knew we were both thinking that unlike his father, my dad *cared* that I came back alive.

I didn't tell Jess that Dad would understand. I think Jess liked to believe that no one knew what his dad was like. But my mom and Jess's mom were good friends. I was sure my parents knew as much–if not more–than I did about their situation.

I sat on the arm of our couch—still in my pajamas but with a hooded sweatshirt thrown on top—right next to Dad. I could feel the warmth of his shoulder as I leaned into him. He stared at the television and laughed along with the audience on the set as David Letterman announced his number seven of the top ten rejected James Bond gadgets. Still chuckling, my dad patted my knee. "What's up, Gemma?" Then looking at his watch, said, "Shouldn't you be in bed?"

"Dad?" I said before he could dwell on the time. "I know I need to go to bed, and I'm going to go soon. And I'm going to make sure that even though I need to stay up a little bit late tonight that I'm going to wake up on time tomorrow morning and be in a really good mood at breakfast, and I'm going to be extremely alert during class." I had asked Dad permission to stay up late enough times to know every excuse why he thought I shouldn't. He began to speak, but I continued before he had a chance, "And even though it may take some strong determination to do those things on less sleep, I know it will be worth it—and I think you'll agree—since it's for a good cause."

Dad opened his mouth and then clapped it together with a smile. "And what—if my attorney general daughter will allow me to ask—is this 'good cause' that is keeping you up past your bed time?"

"It's Jess."

Dad sat forward and twisted to look around the room. "Is he here?"

"He's outside."

"Why is he outside?"

My face fell. While the rest of my speech up to this point was a bit scripted, exaggerated, and even manipulative, the expression on my face now was nothing but sincere. Dad sat back into the couch with an, "oh." He stared back at the television, but he wasn't laughing anymore. He didn't even appear to be paying attention to what was on the screen. He rubbed his hand down both sides of his face and scowled. "Well, your mom went to bed early with a headache, so you'll have to be quiet, but why don't you invite Jess into the house?"

I watched my dad carefully. He looked deep in thought. I was never allowed to have friends over past eight o'clock on the weekdays. This was a big exception. "Yeah, that's a good idea. Thanks, Dad." He nodded, and I got up carefully from the couch before he could change his mind.

I opened the back door and cupped one hand around my mouth. "Come on in, Jess. My dad said it was okay."

Jess turned around to face me. He was obviously surprised at the invitation. Jess didn't come inside my house very often. He came over more when we were little kids and would imitate scenes from *Star Wars* in my basement. But over the past few years we just talked outside. Jess looked up at my house as though it was a huge ship that he was terrified to board. He took a step backward. "I'm okay out here."

I scowled at Jess's hesitation. "What's the matter? It's cold out here." It was only September, but it smelled like it was going to rain. And the breeze brought a chill to my skin.

Jess blinked his eyes a few times. "Just come out here, please?"

I puffed out an exaggerated breath of air and stepped out into the cold. We sat down on our usual spot on the steps while Jess tossed an old basketball around in his hands.

We hadn't said a word to each other before Jess hugged the ball into his chest and announced, "My parents are getting divorced."

I was stunned by his words—especially the unemotional way in which he said them. Jess rarely told me anything about his parents anyway, and this was big. I wasn't quite sure how to react. The first words that came to my mind were *I'm sorry*, but I wasn't sure if that was the appropriate thing to say right now. Before I could do anything, Jess continued, "It's not that surprising; my mom has been threatening for a long time." Jess bent down and dribbled the ball between our feet. I was still at a complete loss for words. Jess shrugged. "Anyway, he's moving out this Saturday, and I'm going to go stay with him for the weekend."

"You're what?" I shouted louder than I meant to at ten o'clock at night.

"Shhh." Jess waved his hand in the air. "It's not a big deal. He's just renting an apartment in West Chester. I'll be back Sunday afternoon."

"Why would you go stay with *him?* He's a bad person."

"He's really only bad when he's been drinking, and I doubt

he'll take off to any bars or liquor stores if it's just me and him in the apartment."

"Why are you going? Why are you taking his side?"

Jess jerked his head to look at me. There was a fire in his eyes I had never seen before. "I'm not taking his side, Gemma." Each word was separated and exaggerated. "I—would—never—take—his—side."

I recoiled at his fierceness but still couldn't understand why he was going to go spend the whole weekend with a man who had made his family's life so miserable. "Why are you going then?"

"Because he asked me to. And my mom thinks it's a good idea for us not to be difficult about spending time with him. Otherwise she's afraid that he'll take us to court. She figures that he'll grow apathetic about being with us over time. Pretty soon he'll be out of our lives for good."

I remembered seeing a movie about this. In the movie, even though the kids hated their dad, the court ordered him to have visiting rights twice a month, and they had to go with him. "But your dad is an alcoholic!" That was the first time I had said it out loud to Jess, even though I always assumed he knew that I knew. "How could he ever deserve visiting rights if he's an alcoholic?"

"We just don't want to make a big deal of it. We don't want any problems."

"But he's mean!"

"Yeah, he is." That was the first time Jess had admitted it. "But he's never really hit us or anything like that, so really it won't stand up for much in court."

A load was lifted off my shoulders. I had always worried so much that he was physically hurting Jess and his mom and sisters. I dropped my shoulders in defeat. I never knew anyone who had parents that were divorced. It was always just something that was talked about in movies and magazines, but not in real life. It was a strange reality. My stomach cramped when I thought of that word, *divorce.*

I finally looked him in the eye and asked, "Are you okay?" It wasn't like Jess to think about himself at a time like this. But I went out on a limb, hoping that he might open up.

Jess cleared his throat. "I'm worried about my mom. I think it's hard on her knowing that us kids won't have a father around." It was so like him to direct the attention from himself and put it on his mom. He spun the basketball between his hands. "But as far as I'm concerned, we've never had much of a father anyway."

I looked at the ground and nodded. I tried imagining what it would be like to not have my dad. That was an awful thought. But just like Jess had said, even when his dad was at home, he wasn't much of a father. Jess and I were living in two different worlds. Jess sighed then tossed the basketball over to the cement pad at the corner of my backyard where the ten-year-old basketball stand was.

I watched the ball roll around and eventually rest next to the fence. Neither one of us spoke for a while, so I hesitantly changed the subject. "I decided today that I need a new group of school friends."

Jess leaned his head on his fist and looked at me from the corner of his eye. For the first time that night he looked amused.

"Really? What brought you to this conclusion?"

I folded my arms and leaned into Jess for some warmth. "I don't know. I never see Clarissa or Nina anymore. But I was getting sick of them anyway. We're just maturing at a different rate. We don't have a lot in common."

Jess laughed out loud.

"What's so funny?"

He shook his head. "I just love the way you are so acutely aware of your maturation level." He wiped his nose—his eyes still squinting with humor. "It's so cute."

I nudged him in the arm with my fist then wrapped my own arm in his and squeezed as close to him as I could.

"So," he continued, "have you found any prospects? Are there any kids that are *maturing* at the same rate as you?"

I let out a discouraged sigh. "Not really. I may be stuck with Clarissa and Nina until I graduate from high school."

Jess shook his head. "Not possible. Even when you have friends that you *want* to keep—it's hard to stay close through-out the years. There are so many new kids coming in from other schools. There are so many different class schedules and activities to be a part of. You naturally drift away from your best friends and start hanging out with the kids that you're around the most."

I looked up at Jess. His face was so close to mine. "What about you and me?" I whispered. "Are we going to drift apart?"

Jess met my questioning eyes, and I could feel his cool breath on my lips. "No. We'll never drift apart. You need me too much." Then his face squinted into the smile that I always loved the most. The smile that I felt I owned and never, ever wanted to give away.

Jess looked down at my shivering hands. "I better take off. You're freezing."

I loosened my tight grip on his arm, and we both stood up to our feet. Jess yawned as he stepped off my porch and looked back up at my house with a thoughtful expression. "You want to know why I didn't want to go inside your house tonight?"

I stood quietly next to him, waiting for him to continue.

He looked back down at me with his tired, sad eyes. "I was afraid that if I went in, I would never want to leave."

I returned his sad expression and wished that there was something more I could do to help him. I couldn't imagine what it must have felt like for him to not want to go home.

Jess began to cross the grass toward the side of my house, but before he left he turned around once more.

"Gem, maybe you could try to just be a normal ninth grader tomorrow, huh? No big catastrophes." He chuckled lightly into the night air.

I sauntered tiredly toward my back door. "When are you going to realize that I'm *not* normal, Jess?"

He started leaving again, and as he did he said, "I take it back." He was still laughing softly, but there was a seriousness to his tone. "Don't change a thing."

chapter nine

The next day at school was uneventful, as was the day after that, and the day after that. Nina waved at me from her new group of friends for the first week or so of school, but eventually the wave became a head nod, and even that eventually disappeared. The deterioration of our friendship was two-sided, though. I made as much of an effort to keep it going as she did. I usually crossed paths with Clarissa about twice a week. She was locker partners with a girl who wore black fingernail polish and baggy pants. Eventually Clarissa started to look just like her and the three other girls they hung out with. By mid-October we could pass each other in the hall without even realizing it. Going through a whole day of school barely talking to anyone wasn't a big deal anymore. In fact, it happened more often than not.

For the first few months of school I avoided going to my locker as much as possible. I decided that the only thing that could make it more impossible for me to make friends was to be seen hanging out in the eighth-grade hall. Unfortunately, I had a massive science project due in third period, and unless I wanted to lug it around with me through all my classes, I was going to have to make the voyage to my loser of a locker.

I kept my head down toward the ground the entire time I was in the eighth grade hall. I figured maybe this way no one would notice me and it would be as though I was never there. I had never been to my locker before, so I still had to look at the tiny piece of paper I was given with the locker number and combination. I peered from the corner of my eye at the lockers until I came to the one that was assigned to me. With my head still down, I hurried to the locker and hastily turned the lock according to my jotted down combination. I was still staring at the floor and about to open my locker when a familiar pair of shoes appeared no more than a foot away from me. The shoes were white running shoes–Nike brand– with gray accents and a green Nike logo on the side. I knew those shoes anywhere. They belonged to Trace Weston.

What in the world was Trace Weston doing in the eighth grade hall? He was one of the most popular guys in school! I slowly peeked up at him from just beneath my eyebrows, and sure enough it was Trace. He was standing at an open locker just two down from mine, unloading his backpack.

It wasn't like this was the first time I had seen him all year. We had second-period German together. But I of course had never said anything to him, not with the way he had rejected me at last year's Valentine's dance. And I was sure he thought I was a total loser and wanted to have nothing to do with me. I quietly stuffed my project into my locker, hoping–more out of habit than out of real desire–that he would say something to me. But he never did. He zipped up his backpack, threw it over his shoulder, closed the locker, and walked away.

I grew anxious for the holidays. They were something to look forward to, even when everything else in my life was uninteresting.

The four weeks before Christmas dragged on slowly. Yet as much as I wanted Christmas day to arrive, I dreaded its coming. As soon as Christmas was here, it was almost over, and so was the magic. Christmas morning came too quickly, leaving Bridget sneaking down the stairs at the crack of dawn—even before my parents were awake—to look at her presents. I would never sneak down early. I wanted to prolong that final moment of seeing all the presents magically laid out as long as I possibly could. Bridget never saw anything anyway. My parents were smart enough to not put out the most special, unwrapped gifts until they had woken up, shooed Bridget back up to her room, set up the tree and stockings, and made the final touches. Only then did they allow us to come downstairs to officially start Christmas.

When the time finally arrived, I held tightly to the banister and closed my eyes. I didn't want to see anything until I was standing in the midst of the magic and could breath it all in. Bridget ran down in front of me and squealed at her presents. When I was seven and she had run down in front of me, she had yelled excitedly, "Gemma, you got a bike!" I cried for twenty minutes over the surprise being spoiled. She never made that mistake again. When I finally felt the landing underneath my slippered feet, I uncovered my eyes to see the most beautiful room in the whole world. It was hard to believe that it was the same old living room I saw every day when I walked down the stairs. Mom had lit candles on top of the fireplace, and the fireplace itself was burning perfectly bright. Dad had turned on Christmas music, and "The Little Drummer Boy" was playing on the stereo system that Mom had given him last Christmas. I could smell cinnamon sticks and clover simmering on the stove in the kitchen, and the carpet even felt softer than usual as it squished beneath my feet. The tree shimmered, and the new twinkle lights Mom had put on it just two weeks before made it come alive. To add to the perfection of the room, the window behind the Christmas tree was slightly frosted as big puffy snowflakes covered the ground outside, leaving a beautiful blanket of white.

When all the presents were torn open and the magical room had suddenly turned into a war zone of ribbons and tissue paper, we slowly moved into the kitchen, where my dad made us all omelets and hash browns while Mom poured us steaming hot chocolate with whipped cream on top. When breakfast was over and the house was quiet, I knew I only had an hour or so before my grandparents and everyone else in our family showed up. Dad was sitting at the kitchen counter with Mom as they tried to figure out the new laptop computer he had given her. And Bridget was in the living room taking the tags off all of her new clothes. This was my one chance to give Jess his present. I quietly crept to the front closet, grabbed my coat, hat, and mittens, and snuck out of the house without being seen. I ran lightly across our snow-covered front yard toward Jess's house, toting a brown package in my left hand. It was still snowing, so I held my hand up in front of my face to shield the flurries from getting into my eyes. The snow was coming down hard now, and it was impossible to see more than two feet in front of me. There was a shocking difference between the cold, brisk morning air and the thrilling warmth that I had just left.

I watched the ground in front of me as I trudged through the cold wetness, making sure to not trip on the curb that led me into the street and the next curb that led me to Jess's front yard. As I worked my way across the snow in front of Jess's house, a sharp, flashing red light just to my left caught my eye. I stopped walking as I squinted in the direction of the light. A strong gust of wind blew, and a million tiny snowflakes floated away in a miniature cyclone across the snow, clearing my view of the red light for an instant. In that moment, I saw a black-and-white police car—the flashing red lights silently blaring on top of it as though someone had hit the mute button. The police car was parked in Jess's driveway. The motor was running, but it didn't look like anyone was inside the car. I stood frozen, piecing together the sight before me when I heard a screen door slam shut in front of me. Through the blustering snow I could make out the image of a large male police officer standing just outside of the screen door, looking down at something in his hand. He didn't seem to have noticed me standing twenty feet away from him. I was still squinting at him through the snow when he lifted his gaze toward me.

"May I help you?"

His voice was grim and the expression on his face was serious. My stomach wrenched in pain.

"I—I'm looking for Jess. Is he here?"

The police officer took a deep breath and lowered his hands to his sides. "Are you related to the family that lives here, young lady?"

I motioned toward my house without losing eye contact with the police officer. "No. I live across the street. I have a present for Jess." I squeezed the package and wondered if the man I was talking to even knew who Jess was. I tucked the package away in my coat.

"Well, the boy's not here," he spoke matter-of-factly and

looked back down at his clipboard, which he was now resting on his large belly.

"Where is he?" My voice sounded loud. I sensed that the police officer would have preferred that I just left.

He didn't look up. "Sorry, ma'am, but I can't give you any details. Not unless you're family."

My heart was racing, and an uninvited pressure started pulsating against my neck. "Is he hurt?" My voice choked on the words.

The officer lowered his hands and the object he had been examining once again and then looked around himself as though making sure that we were alone. He stepped off the porch toward me into the falling snow and then stopped when he was a foot or so in front of me. He spoke this time in a much lower tone.

"Your friend is all right, but his mother is hurt. They're both at Mountain Lakes Medical Center." He stood up a little straighter and checked his surroundings once more. He looked at me with piercing but kind eyes. I nodded my head and turned toward my house. I ran as fast as I could over the same footprints I had made just moments ago. This time, however, I made only half the amount of prints as I leaped toward my front door.

chapter ten

Forty minutes later, Mom and I walked through the revolving doors into the main lobby of Mountain Lakes Medical Center. The roads were slick, so we had to drive slower than usual. It was the longest car ride of my life. I eagerly stepped to the front desk and asked the receptionist where we could find Caris Tyler. The receptionist was older—in her fifties maybe—and she looked tired and not happy to be working on Christmas morning. She looked at me wryly as though a fifteen-year-old girl in a hat, scarf, and mittens had no business talking to her.

Mom assessed the situation and stepped toward the desk. "Yes, we're looking for our friend Caris Tyler. She was brought in this morning—we believe."

The receptionist showed no more kindness toward Mom than she did to me. "What was she brought in for?"

"We're not sure," Mom answered sheepishly. She remained calm and friendly despite the receptionist's disrespectful demeanor.

"Is she having a baby? Or surgery? Tonsils? Gall bladder? Hysterectomy? This is a big hospital, and we have a lot going on in here."

"No, she's not here for surgery. We're not sure what happened, but the police were at her house this morning, so there could have been some sort of an emergency." I could tell Mom was growing impatient, but she forced herself to maintain a calm voice. "Do you have any way of telling us where someone might be by just knowing their name?"

The receptionist cleared her throat and defiantly turned toward the computer in front of her. It was just our luck to have to deal with someone so rude on Christmas morning. I swear that lady must have looked at that computer for five minutes before saying another word. She finally cleared her throat again, and without looking up from the screen, she said, "Tyler, Caris." She pronounced it wrong. She pronounced the first part of her name like a car that you drive. "Looks like she's in the ICU on the third floor."

I didn't know what the ICU was, but I could feel Mom tense up beside me. Her voice was shaking but also demanding as she asked, "Where is the nearest elevator?"

The receptionist—now showing the slightest glimmer of sensitivity—pointed down the hallway to our left. Mom quietly thanked her between her gritted teeth and grabbed my hand hard as she led me toward the direction that we were told to go. When the elevator doors opened on the third floor, a big white sign appeared in front of us with the letters ICU. It didn't take me long to see the words printed just under the letters—*Intensive Care Unit.*

Intensive care? Why was Jess's mom *here?* The nurse that was stationed at the ICU desk was much kinder than the woman in the front lobby. She directed us toward Caris's room, and my breath got lost in my stomach as we approached the door.

Mom looked down at me with weary eyes. "Gemma, why don't you wait out here? I'll take a look and make sure everything is okay, and then I'll come get you, okay?"

I was relieved. I wasn't ready to find out what was behind the closed door. The kind nurse had overheard our conversation and invited me to sit on a chair next to her desk while I waited. There weren't a lot of visitor chairs in the halls in the ICU. I guessed that was because there weren't a lot of visitors allowed in the ICU. The halls were empty, except for another nurse that walked from door to door. I guessed that she was checking monitors and changing catheters, but I couldn't see as the doors shut behind her each time she went in. The nurse at the desk offered me orange juice, but I was too sick to drink anything. I thought about Jess. I wondered if he was behind the same closed door that Mom went into. I sat on the chair for nearly ten minutes before she came back out into the hallway. I looked up at her eagerly, expecting her to wave me over to go into the room. My curiosity and concern were outweighing my nervousness by now, and I so badly wanted to see Jess and know that Caris was going to be all right. Mom's face was pale as she walked toward me. She stooped on the ground next to me and rested her hand on my knee. She looked intensely at the arms of the chair I was sitting on, and I knew she was searching for the words to say.

"Mom?" I broke the silence and my voice cracked. "Is Caris okay?"

Mom's lips pursed together as tears dripped out of her eyes. She shook her head once, and then choked out the words, "She's not doing very well, sweetheart. She's hurt very badly."

"But she's going to be okay?"

Mom just kept right on staring at the arms of the chair.

"Mom? Is she going to be okay?"

"They hope so. That's all they can say right now. She's not conscious."

"What happened to her?"

Mom looked into my eyes for the first time since she came out of the room, and I saw anger blazing from them. She whispered the answer, "Jess's father showed up at their house at four o'clock this morning—intoxicated. He tried taking the girls." She paused for a moment then looked back down again. "I knew they were having some custody issues lately over the holidays and such. Even Caris didn't think he would go this far with it. But there are no limits with Kevin when alcohol is involved." I knew that more than she probably knew I did.

"Where are Viv and Maggie? Are they okay?"

"Yes, they're fine. They're at their grandmother's house."

Vivian and Maggie were Jess's little sisters. They were just seven and ten and much too young to have to experience something like this on Christmas morning. But then again *anyone* was too young to have to experience this on Christmas morning, or any other morning for that matter. I thought of Vivian and Maggie at Caris's mother's house. She was too old to walk let alone give them the happy Christmas they deserved.

"Is Jess here?"

She nodded.

"I don't have to go in there. He probably wants to be alone with his mom."

"He asked if you were here." She squeezed my hand. "He wants you in there with him. He needs you now more than ever."

She stood up and wiped at her eyes. "I'll stay out here. The nurse doesn't want too many people in the room at a time."

I got up from the chair and walked easily toward the door. Knowing that Jess was in there, wanting me to be in there with him, made entering the room a simpler task. But once I was in the room, a whole new reality hit me in the face. I saw Jess sitting next to the one bed in the room, hunched over a bruised and broken body that resembled Caris Tyler. Jess looked up at me when I stepped toward the bed. He smiled faintly, but the smile instantly faded to a look of pain and concern as he looked from me back to his mother. I walked around to the same side of the bed as Jess. As I got closer to him, I realized that he had not left the fight with his dad unscathed. Dried blood was stuck to his knuckles and upper lip. The skin around his eyes and cheekbones was red and almost purple. He was still wearing his pajamas—navy blue sweatpants and a gray hooded sweatshirt—that were covered in blood stains. Probably some of his own blood, and I guessed a lot of his mom's as well—I hoped some of it was his dad's. I had no idea what to say to him. There were no words that could come out of my mouth at that moment that wouldn't sound naïve, insensitive, and apathetic. I sat in the chair next to him and leaned in so closely that I could feel the heat radiating off his back as he hovered over his mother, holding her hand and gently caressing her brow. I had no words, so I simply put my hand on his arm. It was the only way I knew how to tell him that I was there for him. He placed his scarred hand on top of mine. He squeezed it so hard, I thought our two hands might mold together like clay. His breathing became heavy, and then for the first time in my life I saw Jess cry.

When the nurse came into the room, Jess straightened up and wiped his tears on the back of his sleeve. It was the same nurse that I had seen going door to door, and now that I saw her up close I noticed that she was young and pretty looking. Without saying a word, she walked around Caris's bed toward the monitors that were beeping in the corner. She looked really young. She had to still be in high school. I figured that she was probably not a real nurse but one of those volunteers that come in on Christmas to help out. I caught her stealing a glance at Jess when he wasn't looking. From the corner of my eye I saw her look down at our hands then back again at the monitors. She fiddled around with some of the tubes and wrote something down on a clipboard. She quietly asked Jess if he needed anything and then slipped out the door as elegantly as she had entered. When the door shut behind her, Jess spoke the first words I had heard from him since I got there.

"You shouldn't be in a hospital on Christmas morning. You should be home with your family, opening presents, and eating your dad's omelets."

"We've already done all that," I said quietly. "It's not Christmas morning anymore; it's almost two o'clock in the afternoon." I sighed. On a normal Christmas day at two o'clock in the afternoon, I would be sitting at our large dining room table eating ham and cheesy potatoes and Mom's special Christmas salad. I would be surrounded by my twelve cousins and plotting out the best hills to go sledding down after dinner. But this Christmas, I was in Jess's world. I figured this was his first Christmas spent in the hospital too, but the feeling of the day was not new to him. And now I was on the front row seat, seeing everything up close. Jess's hand was still resting on mine, and I silently examined the crusted blood on his knuckles. I wasn't sure if I wanted to know, but I still asked, "Mom said your dad came over in the middle of the night drunk?" I said it with a questioning tone, hoping that he would continue the rest of the story. But he sat silently, staring at his mother's face.

"Sorry," I muttered awkwardly. "You don't have to tell me about it if you don't want to."

He didn't take his eyes off his mother. "I haven't talked about it since it happened. Viv had to tell the police everything because I couldn't." His voice broke, and I thought he was going to cry again, but he didn't. He took a deep sigh and continued, "It was horrible, Gem. I'm afraid the thought of it will haunt me for the rest of my life. I mean, I know he's always had issues, but he's my dad, you know? And to walk in and see your dad doing such terrible things to your mom—to someone who was his wife for eighteen years…"

Eighteen years. That was longer than I had been alive. It occurred to me then that while I had only seen Jess's father a couple times, Jess had seen him every morning when he woke up and every night when he went to sleep. He had eaten dinner at the same table as him for the past sixteen years of his life. Kevin didn't drink all the time, so there were probably times when he was a semi-normal father. He was the one holding the video camera on Christmas morning. The one who stayed up until midnight the night before putting together Viv and Maggie's doll house so that it would be perfect when they saw it the next morning. He was Jess's dad and Caris's husband for eighteen years. He loved them once—maybe he still did—and Jess loved him—maybe he still did. I couldn't begin to imagine what Jess had gone through at those early hours of the morning when I was tucked safely in my warm house—my parents asleep in their bed two doors down the hall.

Jess breathed deeply and let out a long puff of air. Still clenching my hand in his, he removed it from his arm and held it in his
lap as he leaned back in his chair, slumping like a tired teenager
in a first-period geometry class. He closed his eyes for probably
the first time since four o'clock that morning.

"I heard something in the middle of the night, some kind of
scratching sound. I thought I should go check it out, but I was so
tired. The neighbor's cat comes and scratches on our back door so
much; I just figured that was what the sound was, and I fell back
asleep." He ran the hand that wasn't holding mine through his
hair. He looked so tired. "I have no idea how much time passed
before I woke up again to Maggie's screaming. I ran down the
hall to their room and saw my dad holding Viv tightly around her
shoulders while covering her mouth. Maggie was sitting on the
bed crying and begging him to let go of her. I've never seen her so
scared. I've never seen any of us so scared." Jess's eyes were open
now, and he was gazing up into nothingness. It was as though the
whole experience was being projected onto the white ceiling and
Jess was giving me a play by play as he watched it before him. "I
had no idea what to do. I wanted to attack him, but he's my dad.
I ran toward him and pulled Viv from his clenching hands. It
was easier than I thought, and he kind of tripped to the side as
I pulled her away from him. He was obviously drunk, but not so
much that he didn't know what he was doing. He yelled at me.
He told me to go to my room—like I was still ten years old and
I had just come home with a bad report card. I obviously didn't
go to my room; instead I begged him to leave. I didn't know what
else to do, so I just stood cowardly in front of my drunk father
and begged him to leave us alone. That's when my mom came in.
She told me to take Viv and Mags into my room and close the

door. She said she would handle it. I didn't want to go. I didn't want to leave her, but she wanted me to protect the girls. So I did as she said. I took them into my room, and I tucked them into my bed. I knelt on the floor by my bedroom door and listened to them talk. My mom tried to stay calm, but my dad was yelling as she led him downstairs and toward the back door. Their conversation grew faint as they got farther away, so I got up to check on the girls. They were holding each other under my covers, and they were both crying. That's when I heard odd sounds coming from downstairs. I left the girls in my room and ran downstairs as fast as I could. I found my dad standing over my mom, who was curled up in a ball on the floor. I ran toward him just as he smashed one of our solid oak dining table chairs over her back. He raised the chair to do it again, but I intervened. I don't know how many times he hit her before I got there."

Jess wasn't crying anymore. His eyes were emotionless, his face stone cold. He looked numb. Minutes passed before either one of us said anything. The silence in the room made Caris's condition seem that much worse. I'm sure there was much more to the story than Jess had the energy to tell me, but he finished with, "The rest is a blur. The next thing I knew, you were sitting here next to me, and I was crying like a baby."

I held my free hand around my ribs. It felt cold in the hospital room with its white walls and the metal bed. I thought about my warm, picturesque living room with the fire popping and the Christmas tree lights twinkling. How I wished that Jess and I were sitting together there, looking at all our presents rather than his bruised and hurting mother. I hated alcohol. I hated mean people. I hated Jess's dad.

The door to Caris's room opened slowly, and Mom's head peered around the side. "How is she?" she whispered as she floated into the room as lightly as a feather.

Jess was the one that answered, "No change that I can tell. I hope she wakes up soon. She'll be sad if she wakes up and Christmas is over."

Mom sighed sadly. "She'll just be happy to see that you and the girls are all right. It won't matter what day it is."

Jess nodded.

Mom then turned to me. "Gemma?" The sound of her saying my name was strange to me. I was in a whole other world in this cold white room on this particular day of the year, and the sound of my name brought me back to reality.

She continued, "I just talked to your dad. The whole family just showed up at our house. I feel like I need to run home and see them for a little while. Do you want to come with me?"

"And leave Jess?" The idea was barbaric to me.

Jess quickly interjected, "You should go, Gemma."

I whipped my head around. "What? Why?"

Jess spoke slowly, "It's Christmas. You don't have to spend the whole day in this depressing hospital. Go home, see your family. Eat pie and open presents. Laugh. Have fun." His eyes wondered sadly toward the space above my head. I wished I knew what he was thinking about.

I protested, "Christmas will come again next year. And I can see my family another day. They don't live that far away."

"Gemma," Mom interrupted, "Jess may just want a little time alone. Some time to rest."

Jess looked at me. "Some rest would be nice." He squeezed my fingers lightly and I remembered that we were holding hands–in front of Mom.

I leaned in closer to him, my face fixed in a pained expression. "You want me to leave?"

His eyes were sad. He really did look so tired. "I never *want* you to leave, Gem. But I probably should take a nap. The nurse said she'd bring me a cot so I could stay in here with my mom."

Mom's voice broke the silence between us, "I'll bring you back first thing tomorrow morning, sweetheart." Her voice was irritating. I knew she meant well, but I didn't want to leave Jess, and I was growing angry at him for kicking me out.

I stood up quickly from the chair and grabbed my coat, which I had thoughtlessly draped on the end of Caris's bed a half hour before. I was angry and hurt. Hurt that Jess didn't want me to stay and angry at myself for being so self-absorbed at a time like this. My dad used to say that I wore my emotions on my sleeve. For years I thought he meant that my mood determined the shirt I wore that day. If I was happy I wore yellow, sad I wore gray. But what he meant was that I was a terrible fake at hiding my true emotions. And if there were two people in the world that knew me well enough to see right through me, it was Mom and Jess. Usually Jess would have teased me about being so energetic in my distaste for life. But he said nothing. I didn't blame him, though. My attitude problem was hardly an issue compared to the rest of the things he was dealing with. I took a deep breath and swallowed the ball of pride that was rising in my throat.

"Is it okay if I come back tomorrow morning?"

Jess nodded and his face relaxed. "You *better* come back tomorrow."

Later that night, I sat snuggled up on the couch in front of the fireplace while my cousins exchanged gifts. But my attention wasn't on my cousins or even the gift that my cousin Becky—who had chosen my name for the gift exchange—had placed in my lap. I was watching Dad, who sat on the oversized recliner in the back of the room. He had a cup of eggnog in one hand, and he gestured with the other while explaining to my uncle Jack the ins and outs of hardware. Dad worked in an accounting office, but his true love was tools and anything that had to do with tools. Uncle Jack—the artist of the family—seemed disinterested, but he kindly allowed Dad to prattle on about his favorite hobby. I watched the corners of Dad's eyes. I was fascinated by them. When he smiled, a dozen tiny little lines formed at their outer corners. But the fascinating part was that even when he wasn't smiling—like when he was concentrating on his explanation of the different kinds of wrenches—the lines were still there. I realized that Dad smiled so much that he had permanent little lines embossed in his skin.

Mom interrupted my thoughts. "Gemma, honey, aren't you going to open Becky's gift?" She was looking at me with sad eyes, knowing that I wasn't enjoying this Christmas evening with the family as much as I normally did. I nodded and carefully unwrapped the paper on the present. Inside was a tiny little cardboard box filled with rolls of Life Savers. Any other year I would have thanked Becky for her gift, secretly wondering if it was a last-minute re-gift when they remembered they hadn't gotten me anything. But tonight it was exactly what I needed.

I glanced around the room at Bridget and my cousins, completely absorbed in their gift opening. I overheard my mom telling someone about Caris. I thought about Jess and his mom in the hospital. It seemed like they were in a different world. It was like I had fallen asleep after breakfast and the whole thing was just a bad dream. I felt a twinge of guilt for being so comfortable and warm and surrounded by so many people that loved me when Jess was all alone, on a cot, waiting for his mother to wake up. Why did I get such a great dad when Jess got such a terrible one? Why was his mother in the hospital when mine was two feet away from me filling everyone's cups with eggnog and apple cider? My life seemed so simple compared to Jess's. In church they always said that life was a test. If that was true, then why was Jess's test so much harder than mine when we were both just trying to get to heaven?

I knocked on Caris's door at eight o'clock the next morning. An unfamiliar nurse opened the door a crack. She was stern. "We don't allow visitors in the ICU," she whispered and then looked behind me. "Are you alone?"

Before I could explain that my mother was parking the car, I heard Jess's voice deep inside the room. "It's okay, she's family."

The nurse hesitantly let me inside the room. Jess was standing next to Caris's bed; his arms folded tight, his eyes narrow.

I stepped to his side and whispered, "Hi." It sounded like a stupid thing to say in this place.

Jess took a deep breath and nodded at me. I didn't blame him for not saying hi back. It seemed as inappropriate as saying "good morning." I walked toward him but stopped when he jumped. "Nurse!" he spoke directly. "The numbers on this monitor are all over the place. Is that bad?"

The nurse, who had been standing by the door writing something on a clipboard, ran to the monitor almost as immediately as he had spoken. "Everything's fine. This is actually a good sign. It means that she is starting to breathe on her own. She may wake up soon, and it will be best if there are as few people as possible in the room when she does." She looked at me when she spoke.

Jess was watching his mother so intently that I wasn't sure he even heard what the nurse had said.

"I'll wait out in the hall," I said.

Jess glanced at me for a moment then whipped his head back to look at the monitor, where his attention stayed until I exited the room.

Four long hours—and a terrible lunch in the hospital cafeteria—later, Mom and I were finally allowed in Caris's new room on the second floor of the hospital. Caris was awake and sitting up in her bed, but she resembled a corpse with its eyes opened. She looked older and younger at the same time. Older because her hair was matted to the back of her head and large circles appeared under her eyes where the bandages weren't covering; younger because she seemed so small and fragile—so vulnerable. Caris was born in Ireland, which explained the tint of red in Jess's brown hair, but lived in Franklin most of her life. For the most part she had the usual American accent, but for some reason today there was a hint of Irish in her voice.

"Hi, ladies." Her voice was hoarse, and I could barely make out what she said. She almost lifted a finger to wave at us but then seemed to change her mind at the last minute. "Thank you for coming."

My mom placed her hand on Caris's bandaged hand. "How are you feeling?" She had a way of making the most common question sound truly heartfelt and sincere.

"Blessed."

Caris's answer was short, but it took me back. Blessed? Her? She just spent Christmas day unconscious and wired to a hospital bed because her ex-husband beat her with a dining room chair, and she felt blessed?

She continued slowly, "I can't say I wasn't disappointed that I missed Christmas, but I trust that you drank some eggnog for me." Caris was particularly spry considering her condition, and I wondered how much painkiller was being pumped into her veins right now. I exchanged a glance with Jess, who was sitting on a sofa against the far wall, that told me he was wondering the same thing. I let Mom and Caris continue their conversation as I slowly inched my way toward the sofa. I sat down carefully next to Jess. I was worried that if I got too close to him he would crack down the middle.

His first words surprised me. "Sorry about this morning." I jerked my head to look at him. What did he possibly have to be sorry about? "I didn't have a chance to say much to you." I didn't think it would be necessary to remind him that he had said nothing to me. "I really appreciate you coming, though. Even though you were just out in the hall, it meant a lot to me."

I nodded but said nothing. I thought he'd appreciate the silence. We sat quietly on the sofa for another twenty minutes while our moms talked. Eventually I heard Caris ask my mom, "Could you take Jess home for me? He needs to get some sleep before he ends up in the bed next to me."

"Of course," Mom replied, "but he'll be alone at your house. Why don't we take him to our home or to your mother's house with the girls?"

Caris shook her head. "Mom can't take on another one. She called a minute ago and said that the girls were already more than she can handle. She just got hip surgery, you know. I told her that Jess would be more of a help than a hinder but—," she looked at Jess sadly and opted not to finish the sentence. "He'd have to sleep on the couch there anyway. It would do him some good to sleep in a nice comfortable bed."

Jess entered the conversation, "Mom, let me stay here with you. This cot is fine for me." He leaned forward and patted the edge of a cot that looked big enough for a small child to fit on it.

Caris shook her head. "No it's not, Jess. You need sleep and a good meal. Besides, the doctor says I'm stable. You can come back and see me tomorrow."

"But Mom—"

"Not another word, Jess. I may be all battered and bruised up, but I'm still your mother, and I want you to go with Suz and Gemma."

She sounded like she was talking through a straw, but Jess still recoiled into the couch. Then she added, "How about you and Gemma head out to the car. There's something I need to talk to Suzanne about."

Jess and I walked sluggishly out of the hospital room like two kids that had just been punished. But as the door closed behind me, I could hear Caris starting to cry.

chapter eleven

I was setting plates on the table when Jess shyly walked into our kitchen. His hair was wet, and he was wearing a set of my dad's sweats. I was amazed at how well they fit him.

My mom looked up from grating the cheese. "Jess, are you sure there's not a spare key to your house under a mat or rock somewhere?"

"No, my mom never hides keys outside. She's always home."

We had been driving up our lane when it donned on Jess that he didn't have the key to his house. He had left so quickly to catch up with the ambulance that he didn't even think about it. And of course the cops didn't either.

"Well, Rob's clothes are just going to have to work until we find another solution."

It was three o'clock in the afternoon, an awkward time for either lunch or dinner. But Mom and I had only picked at the stale pizza we ordered at the hospital—and I had no idea when Jess ate last—so we were practically starving. Dad and Bridget, who had already eaten, sat at the table with us to hear about Caris's con-

dition. It only took about five minutes for Jess to explain everything about his mom, and then the conversation—to Jess's relief—
turned to lighter subjects like Christmas presents and New Year's
Eve plans. It was strange having Jess over for dinner. As often as he
came to our house, he had never come in for dinner or even hung
out with the rest of my family much before. It was strange mixing
the two universes—the family universe and the Jess universe—but
it was oddly comfortable at the same time. Jess and Dad gabbed
most of the time about baseball while Mom and Bridget planned
the post-Christmas shopping spree. After the dishes were all done,
Mom told me to move some clothes and things I needed over the
next few days into Bridget's room so that Jess could have mine. I
knew he felt uncomfortable about the arrangement, but I loved the
idea of having him stay with us for a while.

Jess sat at the desk in my room while I threw three days'
worth of clothes into a pile on my bed. He was especially quiet
tonight, but I had plenty of things to tell him to fill the silence.

"Do you know Mike Hodgins?" I didn't wait for him to
answer. "He's a senior, and he has a big crush on Bridget."

Jess nodded as he opened one of the drawers of my desk.

"Well, the night before Christmas Eve, the doorbell rang and
it was Mike Hodgins and his two best friends—Hal Butters and
some Ian guy." I laughed at the memory. "You wouldn't believe it,
but they were all dressed up as elves! Hal and Ian in velvet green
suits and Mike as Santa Claus!"

Jess looked up at me for a moment and then continued digging through the paraphernalia that was stashed in the drawers.

"So they sang Christmas carols in front of my parents and
me and everything! Then handed her a whole bunch of presents
and left!"

"They just left?" Jess asked as he reached into the back of the middle drawer.

"Yes! But then Bridget followed them outside and talked to them for a while on the driveway."

"Does Bridget like Mike?"

"I think so." I shrugged as I held up two shirts that I was try-ing to decide between. "But it was seriously so funny. You would have laughed so hard."

"What's this?" Jess sat up straight in the chair as he retrieved a brown paper bag from the back of the drawer.

I gasped as I stepped toward him. "I can't believe I forgot!" I grabbed the bag from him. "This is your Christmas present!"

"Then why did you take it from me?" Jess held his empty hands out in front of me.

"Because I worked hard on it, and I want to be able to *give* it to you." I took the wrapped gift out of the brown bag and deli-cately placed it in his hands. "Merry Christmas."

"What? No elves? No song and dance?" Jess chided as he ruthlessly tore off the wrapping paper and dropped it on the ground beside his chair.

He ripped off the lid of the box with as much force but paused instantly when he saw what was inside. His eyebrows squeezed together, and he tilted his head as if trying to figure out what it was.

"Thanks," he said as enthusiastically as he could.

I let out a frustrated puff of air and took the gift out of the box. "It's a scrap book. See?" I opened the cover and began show-ing him the pages inside. "It's just a bunch of pictures, movie tickets, arcade tokens, and stuff that I've kept over the years. See this one?" I pointed to a page about halfway through that had an old crumpled up receipt taped next to a picture of Jess and I arm and arm. "This is a receipt from that creepy witch doctor we met in town a couple summers ago."

Jess opened his mouth as he tried to recall what I was talking about. "Oh yea!" He let out a raspy laugh. "I bought a bottle of old gun powder from her because she said it would give me bigger muscles by just rubbing it on my skin."

I nodded, excited that he remembered. "Yeah, I kept the receipt."

Jess continued to flip through the book, obviously amazed with all the memories it was bringing to his mind. "Our comic strip!" he announced when he got to one of the back pages. It was a five-frame comic strip that we had made up together one rainy summer day when I was ten. It was stupid really, and not funny at all, but it brought back memories of that day. We had been at the lake when it started raining. By the time we ran to my house we were drenched, so we made hot soup and grilled cheese sandwiches and sat around playing monopoly for hours. When we couldn't play monopoly for another second, we made up this comic strip–that at the time we were sure was going to make us famous someday.

"Wait a minute," Jess said, tapping his finger against his upper lip. "This isn't the original comic strip. It wasn't even on paper. Wasn't it written..." He paused and looked around my room as if trying to grasp the memory.

"On my closet wall?" I completed his thought.

He beamed, having remembered it now that I said it. "Is it still there?"

"Yeah, I just copied it down a week ago."

His eyes widened with curiosity. "Can I see it?"

I led him into my tiny box-like, walk-in closet. I pushed a few of my old church dresses apart and crawled between them until I was against the wall. "It's hard to see it in the dark," I explained as I turned and sat against the wall just next to the drawing. "I had to use a flashlight when I copied it down."

Jess crawled in between my dresses until he was stooped right next to me peering at the writing. "It's so tiny!"

"I know. You wanted to make sure no one would ever see it. I think you did a pretty good job."

Jess rubbed his fingers across the tiny letters. After a moment he sighed and swung around until he was sitting right next to me against the wall. He leaned into me as he asked, "When did life get so complicated?" I could feel his body move as he took in another deep breath and then let it out again. The warmth of his shoulder penetrated mine, and I found myself instinctively cozying up to his heat. I thought about the complications of my life. There weren't many. Sure, I didn't have a lot of friends. But I had one best friend that I was truly grateful for. I had a great family. A nice home. All the food I wanted to eat. What more could a girl need? I knew Jess was looking at life from a completely different perspective. I didn't understand it entirely, but I knew his world was a different color than mine.

I didn't respond to Jess's rhetorical question, and neither did he. We sat in silence for a while, until my bedroom door opened and Dad's voice broke the silence.

"Gemma? Jess?"

Startled, I sat straight up and yelled back to him from the closet, "We're in here!" My voice sounded so loud against the four tiny walls.

Dad was in the closet in the next moment as Jess and I scurried from our spot between the dresses.

"What are you two doing," he paused and looked around him as if trying to figure out where he was, "in your closet?" The last part of the question came out with more force and a hint of anger.

Jess and I stumbled to our feet. The closet wasn't big enough for the three of us to be standing without breathing into each other's faces. Dad backed out slowly and stood outside the door with his arms folded, waiting for an answer to his question. I could only imagine what Dad was thinking; Jess and me in the closet, alone. I rolled my eyes at his apparent accusation as I stepped toward him and out of the closet. "Dad," I said as I tamed my frizzy hair, "we were only looking at something that we drew on the wall a long time ago."

Dad looked relieved until his face changed to a different shade of red. "You drew on your *wall?*"

Oops. Jess fidgeted next to me. Dad was usually calm and extremely patient, but when he got mad, you *knew* you were in trouble.

"Dad," I said with a nervous laugh, "it's so small you can barely see it." I searched for the right words to talk us out of this predicament. "Besides, it's a lot better than what you originally thought we were doing, right?"

Dad huffed and grumbled something under his breath. He turned to look at the pile of clothes on my bed, and then he bent down and grabbed them all in one swoop. "Come with me, Gemma," he said through gritted teeth as he walked out the door and into the hall. Then came the punishment. "You're not to step a foot in that room while Jess is staying in this house."

Jess ended up staying at our house for the rest of the holiday break. Mom or dad would drive him to the hospital every day around noon, and that's where he would stay until they picked him up in time for dinner that night. We found out from the police that Jess's dad was arrested Christmas day. He was released a few days later but was being held under strict supervision until his court date, which would be sometime in January.

The night before school started again, Caris was released from the hospital. She still looked haggard when my parents, Jess, and I picked her up. She walked with a limp, and one of her eyes was still swollen shut. When she wanted to turn her head, she had to turn her whole upper body because her neck was so sore. But amazingly enough, she looked happy. Jess looked happy to have her home too, and I was happy that Jess wouldn't have to go to the hospital every day; though a strange pang of sadness crept into my stomach as I watched Jess lead his mom out of our car and up the porch steps to their house. I had gotten so used to having him in the bedroom next door that clear across the street seemed like miles away.

That night as I was in my room cutting out magazine pictures for a school project I had due the next week, I heard an old familiar tapping at my window. I flipped my light on and off as always and ran down the stairs–my heart pounding wildly with every step. I was nearly panting by the time I got out my back door.

"Hey, stranger," I said as I sat next to Jess on the steps.

He looked relieved to see me. "I know. It seems like it's been forever since I saw you last." He rubbed his hands together. "I got used to being around you all the time."

"How's your mom?" I said while hugging my ribs to stay warm. It was an especially cold night, and our breath swarmed around our heads as we spoke.

"She's tired." Jess's eyes seemed distant, and I could tell he hadn't come over to talk about his mom. Jess shifted as he reached into his pocket. "I have something for you."

I leaned forward to see what he was pulling out of his pocket. "What is it?" I asked, trying to decipher the object that was hidden in the bag in his hand.

He handed me the bag. "Merry Christmas."

I held it in my hand and turned it around so I could see it at every angle.

"It's been in my room all this time," Jess explained, "but I couldn't get in my house so...," his words trailed off as I put the bag up to my ear and shook it in order to have a better idea of what it was. Whatever it was made a small rattling sound when I shook it.

"Jess, you shouldn't have," I said in an exaggerated and obviously joking tone. "I've always wanted a container of Tic Tacs for Christmas!"

Jess watched me intently as I played my little game. I loved the fact that I had a secret present in my hand from Jess, and I didn't want that feeling to go away.

"Next year I'm just going to get you a brown paper bag," he said after I made a few more fake guesses. "You're having more fun with *it* than you will with the actual present."

When I couldn't come up with any more guesses, I reached inside the bag and pulled out a small white container that was just bigger than a matchbox. I lifted the lid to find a shiny silver bracelet with a single red gemstone hanging from the end. I carefully lifted it out of the box and let it dangle delicately from my fingers as I examined every inch of it.

"It's a ruby," he said softly. "The guy at the store said it's the most powerful gem in the world." He was quiet for a moment before adding, "Like you."

I carefully rotated the flawlessly cut round ruby between my thumb and my index finger. "It's perfect," I whispered, and then I looked at him for the first time since opening the gift. "Thank you."

Jess's expression was serious. "You're welcome."

I breathed in the freezing cold air and leaned forward to let my head rest in the palms of my hands. "I don't want to go back to school tomorrow." I gazed out at the newly fallen snow that covered my backyard. "I don't want to go back to being alone all day."

Jess rubbed his hand gently over my head. "I have a good feeling about this semester," he said with a low voice. "Things are going to start changing, for the better." He blew into his free hand. "It's about time for a change, I think."

I sat up straight and looked at Jess with a concerned expression. "I don't want things to change between us."

He looked at me and gently took the bracelet out of my hands. He unclipped the end and quietly wrapped it around my wrist. "I didn't get you the most powerful gem in the world just because I think *you're* powerful," he said with a teasing smile.

I watched him closely, waiting for him to finish.

"I got you the most powerful gem in the world because of us." He took my hand in his and twisted the small ruby between his fingers. "Nothing can come between us. No matter what." Then as if it was more of a supplication than a statement, he looked up at me with pleading eyes. "Okay?"

I had never seen Jess like this before. So open. So honest. I felt a little stronger at that moment knowing that he needed me in his life as much as I needed him in mine. And for the first time I felt a glimmer of hope that maybe we actually would be there for each other, always, and no matter what. Jess's fierce eyes softened as I nodded my head, and he handed me back my wrist. "It's late," he said with a sigh. "I should go." He boosted himself up off the step and helped me to my feet. My legs felt frozen, and it was hard to straighten them again. "Have fun tomorrow." He paused and almost without thinking I stepped into him, my head reuniting with his chest once again. He wrapped his arms firmly around me and pressed his cheek against the top of my head.

We held each other for a few minutes more, knowing that as soon as we let go we'd have to part our separate ways. That he'd have to go back to high school and I'd go back to stupid ninth grade. When we finally let go, Jess slid his hand down my hair as it fell over my shoulder. Then he looked behind me at my house. "I knew that once I went in, I wasn't going to want to leave." He let his hand drop to his side.

I cocked my head to one side. "I don't know, after a week and a half of sharing my bathroom and getting killed at monopoly— I'm sure you must be a little sick of me."

I waited for him to twist his face and return my teasing remark. But his eyes remained serious, and his fingers lingered on the tips of my hair as he whispered, "I could never get sick of you, Gemma. It's not possible."

chapter twelve

The first day back at school was as monotonous as the rest. I actually remembered my schedule for the new semester—probably because only two classes actually changed—which only made my day that much more boring. I yearned for a friend that I could walk to class with and hang out with after school. I wanted to go to my locker and find a note from her that had been written in pink pen while she was bored in biology class.

The repetitive days passed quickly, and before I knew it we were two months into the semester. Second period this semester was still German. The late bell had already rung, and I was half walking, half running down the hall toward my class. I was alone in the halls except for one other girl in front of me who was also walking toward my second period classroom—though she appeared to be in no hurry at all. She was noticeably shorter than me, with jet black hair that was slicked back into a ponytail. I recognized her from the back of her head as Drew Markoviak. Drew was that girl in school that started all the latest styles. If

Drew wore a speckled brown long sweater jacket to school, pretty soon the halls were lined with girls wearing some imitation form of a long brown sweater jacket. She was the girl that belonged on the front cover of every teen magazine. She was that sort of tomboyish girl with the perfect body, smothered in mud from the ongoing co-ed rugby game, and surrounded by deliciously handsome boys who looked like they could eat her up for dessert.

Needless to say, Drew was popular. But not the bouncy blond hair, cheerleading kind of popular. Drew was just flawlessly cool without an enemy in the world. She approached the door just before I got there. I slowed down as I neared her, and I tried to conceal my heavy breathing. I was slightly embarrassed that I was trying to hurry to class when she seemed so casual about being late. She opened the door and glanced at me as I approached.

"Hey, Gemma."

She knew my name? I was so shocked that I almost forgot to say anything back. "Um, hey, Drew."

She nodded her head at me then slipped smoothly into the classroom. The teacher, Frau Hart, didn't even turn when she walked across the room and sat at her desk. She probably didn't hear her, as Drew was so quiet and graceful when she slid effortlessly into her seat. The exact opposite happened when I entered. The door slammed shut behind me, and Frau Hart as well as the entire class turned and stared right at me. One person who was watching me particularly closely was Trace Weston. He was holding his pencil to his lips and smiling at me as I loudly and awkwardly walked down the second aisle to my desk, sat down, and pulled out my books. I only kept eye contact with him for a nanosecond, but I could feel him watching me as I settled into my chair.

Frau Hart stopped writing on the chalkboard long enough to frown at me and say, "Tardiness is not tolerated in my class." I wanted to believe that she was talking to both Drew and me, but somehow I knew that wasn't the case. Frau Hart gave us twenty minutes at the end of class to work on our homework. I was closing my eyes, trying to memorize a German poem when I felt a tap on my shoulder. I opened my eyes to see Drew sitting in the vacant seat next to me. I hadn't even heard her sit down.

"Don't worry about Frau *Fart*," she whispered with a crinkled nose.

I looked over my shoulder at Frau Hart, who was busy grading papers at her desk. I had heard some of the kids calling her Frau *Fart* when she was out of earshot, but I didn't know where it had started—until now.

"What are you talking about?" I said nervously as I straightened the papers on my desk.

"You're kidding, right?"

"What?"

"I thought you were going to burst a blood vessel when she nagged you about being late."

I was slightly perturbed that she thought Frau Hart was talking to me alone. Then I thought about my nearly bursting blood vessel and wondered if Trace had seen it too. I shrugged. "I'm fine."

"Seriously, what's the worst that can happen?"

"Uh." I raised my eyebrows. "She can give me a bad grade. She can keep me after for detention. She can call my mom. The lady pretty much owns my life."

"So she drops your grade. Then what?"

The answer seemed obvious. "I get a bad grade."

"Uh huh. And then what?"

I didn't understand the game of questions. Where was she going with this? "And then that bad grade stays on my report card forever."

"Forever?"

"For the next three years until I want to get into college somewhere."

"And you think a half grade drop in your ninth-grade German class is going to stop you from getting into the college you want to get into?"

"I don't know, maybe."

"Let me tell you the correct answer. No. So chill out."

At that she got up from the chair with a wry smile and walked back to her desk and the three girls who seemed startled that she would talk to anyone else but them.

After that Drew started acknowledging me in the halls. She would nod my way or lift her hand in a half wave. Sometimes she verbalized a hello. I was surprised every time, but I usually said hi back. We didn't talk much in class, but I barely noticed. I was too busy trying to figure out the German language. I was so behind, and I hadn't even started my mid-term project, which was due in two weeks.

"Do you have a group for the mid-term project already?" I had been focusing so intently on the vocabulary list I was memorizing that I hadn't seen Drew sit down in the same chair as she had the first time. I should have had a group by this time, but I didn't.

"No. Do you?" Stupid question. Of course she did, she had a permanent group of followers. So why did she ask?

"Yeah, but we need another person. We're making a movie about some German kids living in Eastern Germany post-World War Two. There are only four of us. We need a fifth person.

"You're doing a movie? I thought we just needed to write a story together." The assignment was to—as a group—write about a significant event in German history. And of course it was supposed to be written in German.

"We'll have to write the script down anyway; we're just going above and beyond. Frau Fart will love it."

Frau Fart—I mean Hart—stirred in her chair, and I could have sworn she heard what Drew had called her. I wasn't sure what to do. I wasn't usually a risk taker when it came to homework. I wasn't much of a risk taker at all. But I was even more worried about not having a group for the project at such a late date.

"Sure, I'll do it with you." The words scared me as they came out of my mouth.

Drew looked pleased. "Awesome. We're meeting at my house today after school." She handed me a piece of paper with her address and then got up from the chair. "We'll see you around four then."

"Four." I nodded in agreement while looking at the directions that she had carefully sketched out on the thick piece of yellow note paper. Even her handwriting was careful and decisive. It could have been a fancy font option on Microsoft Word.

"Oh!" Drew said as an afterthought. "If you have any old eighties outfits, bring them. We need all the costumes we can get."

Mom dropped me off at Drew's house at four o'clock sharp. I felt stupid being so exactly on time. When she answered the door, Drew looked down at the heap of clothes in my hands.

"That'll work." She twisted her lips into a half smile. I could tell she was satisfied with the look of uncertainty on my face. "Come on back; everyone else is already here."

Her house was huge and daunting. The ceiling throughout the entire house was at least thirty feet high with windows that reached to the very top. Drew led me into the main living room— which looked like the lounge of a fancy ski resort hotel—and just as she had said, the groupies were already there. I knew all three of them by name, and that was about it. Stella, the tall brunette, was sitting on the floor playing with the stereo. Stephanie, the tiny one with glasses, was sitting cross-legged on an oversized chair playing with her gum, and Carmen, who always appeared to be Drew's most dominant follower, was draped over the couch as though she lived there, flipping through a celebrity magazine.

Drew walked into the room ahead of me and waved her hand back in my direction. "Guys, you all know Gemma." She didn't ask them, she told them. They all acknowledged me as I walked in, and I felt my nerves settle slightly. They didn't seem to be the mean girls in every high school movie that I thought they'd be. They appeared to be just normal people.

Drew looked me up and down. "Are you going to put on your costume?"

I held it up in disgust. "Is this for me to *wear?*" I had hastily grabbed Mom's old prom dress from the costume box in our basement. It was a million different shades of pink with all sorts of ruffles and sequins designs on it.

Drew put both hands on her hips. "Who did you think was going to wear it?"

I took a deep breath and draped the pink ruffles over my head and shoulders. It barely fit. Mom must have been tiny in high school. By the time I got the zipper up, the rest of the girls were finishing off their outfits. Stella, Stephanie, and Carmen all looked like identical eighties cheerleaders. Drew had a humongous Tina Turner-style wig on with a cut off T-shirt and frayed shorts. And I was standing awkwardly in my mom's old prom dress. Drew, who was obviously in charge of the whole operation, stood behind a video camera that was set on a tripod.

"Okay," she said louder than she needed to while looking intently at the camcorder buttons, "take one of *Die Frühstück-Verein auf Deutschland.*" Her German accent was messy, but I could piece together the words she had said from past vocabulary lists. The name of the movie was *The Breakfast Club in Germany.* I laughed out loud as soon as I pieced it together.

Drew looked up at me from behind the camera. "What's so funny?" The other girls watched me in silence.

I uncomfortably tucked my hair behind my ears. "What does *The Breakfast Club* have to do with post-World War Two Germany?"

Drew looked at me with a sincerely confused expression. "World War Two ended in the forties, Gemma."

"Okay?" I waited for the explanation.

"*The Breakfast Club* was in the eighties, which is *after* the forties."

I gasped with laughter once again. But no one else was laughing. Before I had a chance to object—before I had a chance to explain to them that we were all going to fail the mid-term project if we turned in a homemade German version of *The Breakfast Club,* Drew gave Stella the cue to start the music, which was a modern version of "99 Luft Balons" by Nena. The music was loud, and I had no idea what I was supposed to do. No one had given me a script. I stood awkwardly in the middle of the room while Drew and the other three girls danced in front of the camcorder.

"Come on!" Drew whispered. She was smiling widely while whipping her head around in circles. "Dance!"

I started mimicking their eighties dance moves. I followed Carmen as she did the pony, and then I started turning my head in circles like Drew, my long hair whipping around my head and against my closed eyelids. We danced for half of the song until Drew gave Stella the cue to lower the volume so that the song became background music. Drew then waved her hand at Stephanie, who quickly grabbed a poster board from off the couch that read "*Verzögerung*" and held it in front of the camera. I didn't recognize the word.

"What does that mean?" I whispered to Stella, who was standing closest to me.

"Detention."

I gave her a look of confusion.

"That's what *The Breakfast Club* is about. It's about five kids in detention." She whispered it so loudly I was almost positive it would be heard on the camcorder, but I decided that wasn't a bad thing, since anyone watching this movie would be as confused as I was. It was beginning to be clear as to why Drew said they needed another person in their group. There were five kids in detention in the original movie, and I was the fifth kid. Drew and Carmen scurried around, putting five kitchen chairs in front of the camera, then everyone sat down, so I did too. The camcorder never stopped running. Drew said it was more artistic to change scenes while it was still on record. I believed her. The rest of the movie consisted of us all trying to talk to each other like we were angry students in detention. Of course it had to be in German, so the sentences were short and simple and consisted of the few vocabulary words we remembered. A couple of times Drew picked a fight with someone, which eventually turned into a fake fist fight right in front of the camera. The movie ended ten minutes later with us all deciding to be friends and giving each other high fives. Stella turned the song back on, and we all danced again until Drew ran over to the camcorder and yelled cut.

Between the afternoon I spent at Drew's house and the day our project was due, I had a handful of conversations with Drew and her posse, though we talked about little more than our video.

The mid-term project was due the first Tuesday in March. Frau Hart called each group up to the front of the class one group at a time to read their stories to everyone. It was tedious just listening to the other group's stories. For one thing, they were extremely long and boring and full of words that none of us knew! And for another thing, I was agonizing over the humiliation I was going to feel when we had no story, but a completely unsystematic video about an eighty's movie.

"Drew?" Frau Hart peered over her glasses and scanned the room until she spotted our little group. "Your group is next." Frau Hart was all business. I was terrified of what her reaction would be to our movie. I wiped my sweaty hands along my jeans as I stood up to walk to the front of the class. Before I had a chance to move, Drew nudged me and motioned for me to sit down.

"Frau Hart," Drew spoke with confidence, and I didn't understand how she could not be scared of the teacher, "it won't be necessary for my whole group to come up with me. We don't have a story to read." She held up a tiny disc in her left hand. "We took the effort to act out our story and record it onto a DVD. I have it here to show everyone."

We took the effort? The way Drew phrased it even I was convinced that we had done something special. Maybe we would get a good grade after all. But then again, Frau Hart hadn't seen the movie yet. Surely as soon as she saw that it had nothing to do with German's history she'd give us a failing grade. Frau Hart scurried to her feet and rolled the television and DVD player to the front of the room. I was in shock; so far she hadn't said a thing about us not following the assignment. Drew smoothly turned on the equipment and slid the disc in the player.

"Frau Hart, would you mind turning off the light?"

My jaw nearly dropped to the floor as Frau Hart flipped off the light switch and scurried back to her desk to watch the movie. The entire class was staring at the black screen, and I felt nauseated as I thought about that first scene when Drew had first turned on the camera at her house. I had been standing clueless in the center of the room when the music had come on. My awkward and confused face was going to be the first thing that everyone saw. I was going to look like a complete idiot!

But I was wrong again. The first thing to appear on the black screen were words. The first words listed our names. I was surprised to see my name at the top of the list. Then the title of the movie showed in German with the English name in parentheses below it. While the title was still showing, the opening song began. When the actual movie finally started, we were well into our dancing. My awkward stance had been totally skipped over! The whole class watched the five dancing girls with wide, excited eyes. Even Frau Hart had an amused look on her face. The rest of the film looked like a completely different movie than what I had participated in that day at Drew's house. There were distinct cuts and scene changes. There were smooth close-ups of each of us as we spoke. It actually looked like a good movie! I was amazed! And so was the rest of the class. I glanced at Trace once—probably out of habit—to see him leaning forward on his elbows, intently watching the movie. I watched him as his eyes moved around the screen. He had a new expression every time we spoke on the movie. When the movie finally ended, everyone cheered and clapped their hands. Frau Hart was laughing joyfully and even clapped her hands a couple times as she stood up to turn the lights back on.

"*Wundervoll! Wundervoll!*" Frau Hart exclaimed as she rolled the television back to its place behind her desk. "Für deine großen Anstrengungen danke," which in English meant, "Wonderful! For your great efforts, thank you!"

I couldn't believe it. Drew had gotten away with it. We all had gotten away with it! Our project was a hit! I looked over at Drew, who was lounging back in her chair with a slight grin as though it was no particular big deal at all. The next group was called, and I figured that the end of our project meant the end of my friendship with Drew, Stella, Stephanie, and Carmen. I didn't belong with those girls anyway. They had a magic that I couldn't compete with. So I was surprised when I walked out of class when the bell rang and heard Drew yell my name. "Gemma, wait up!"

I stopped in place and turned around as the rest of my German class whizzed by me. I felt some of them looking at me differently, and then I saw Trace. He was walking toward me and looking at me straight in the eyes. I stopped breathing. When he got within six inches of me, he stepped to the side and breezed past me while whispering, "Nice dancing."

Was he serious? Was he mocking me? I couldn't tell. But the smell of his cologne twirled through my hair and around my nose, and the same fluttery feelings that I had about him last year danced inside my stomach once again. Before I had a chance to analyze what had just happened, my elbow was being yanked and I looked down to see Drew at my side.

"Do you know him?"

"What? Who?" I looked around as though I didn't know what she was talking about.

"Trace Weston. Are you friends with him?"

I blew a raspberry through my lips. "Trace Weston and me—friends? Uh, no."

"Hm." She looked at me unconvinced then without skipping a beat asked, "Where's your locker?"

Her question threw me. Did she know that Trace's locker was beside mine? I wasn't sure if I was quite prepared to reveal that hidden treasure. "Uh, it's ..." I pointed toward the eighth grade all.

She looked disgusted. "You're in the eighth grade hall?"

"My family was out of town during registration, so I ... "

She seemed to guess the rest of the story. "You should put your books in mine and Carmen's locker from now on." It was closer to a demand than a suggestion. She started walking down the hall again and I followed.

"Where are the other girls?" I didn't have to say their names. She knew who I was talking about.

She shrugged. "I don't know. They're big girls. They can make it to third period on their own."

She had just finished speaking when the three girls in discussion bounced around us from behind. "Where'd you go?" Stephanie asked as she watched Drew, who barely acknowledged her. Stephanie looked hurt.

"We always wait for *you*," Stella spoke more quietly, like she only meant for us to accidentally overhear what she had said.

Drew didn't respond to either of their complaints. I thought she was mad, but three seconds later she was banging her hands together wildly. "Girls, take a look at Kit Walker!" She pointed toward where he was standing then turned to us with one hand cupping her mouth as she whispered loud enough for us all to hear, "I think he forgot his pants this morning."

Kit Walker was a full-fledged jock. He was captain of the ninth grade basketball team and even dressed for the high school junior varsity team. He was one of the most popular guys in the school. So popular, in fact, that he could get away with running to his locker in only his boxers to grab the gym shorts he had accidentally left there.

"Hey, Kit!" Drew yelled out to him with her contagious and carefree laugh. "You forgot to put on pants today!"

Kit didn't even look up from his locker. He was still rooting around looking for something when he yelled, "Drew! Haven't I told you? Pants are so overrated!" He looked up at us all just as we approached him. He had a huge grin on his face as he slapped Drew's hand and told her he missed seeing her more often. He patted Carmen on the back, as she was the only other girl close to him, and he even looked me in the eye for a moment.

"Seriously though, Kit. Where are your shorts?"

Kit cocked his head back. "I really don't know! I thought they'd be in here." He looked down at his plaid boxer shorts and shrugged. "I guess these will just have to do for gym class today." Then he scurried off to the gymnasium, leaving Drew in a fit of laughter as she continued down the hall.

I followed her to her locker, which I found out was shared by Stella, Stephanie, and Carmen too. The locker was lined with cut out magazine photographs of celebrities and male models, and it smelled like a combination of hairspray and perfume.

"So who do you like, Gemma?" Drew asked it so casually you would have thought she asked what I was having for lunch.

"Who do I like?" I said hesitantly. Jess's face blazed in my mind, and Trace came in as a distant second. But I had made the mistake of revealing my crushes to Clarissa and Nina, and that had been a disaster. I wasn't about to spill the beans now to a girl that I barely knew.

"Do you have a boyfriend?" she urged.

My shoulders fell with a twinge of embarrassment. "No." I was sure that all of them had been kissed at least once by now.

"Who do you like then?"

My heart pounded as Jess's name danced on the tip of my tongue. "No one," I lied as I put my smallest book in the locker.

"Well, you must like someone. What about Trace Weston?"

My stomach fluttered when she mentioned his name. But I puffed out my bottom lip and said, "No."

Drew looked up at me with skeptical eyes. Then her attention was drawn downward. "What about that bracelet. You wear it every day." She cocked her head to one side. "Where did you get it?"

I looked down at the bracelet that Jess had given me and wondered how I was going to escape Drew's line of questioning. "It was a gift," I caressed the dangling ruby with my fingers, "from a good friend." I looked back up at Drew and changed the subject. "How about you? Who do you like?"

Drew beamed with wide excited eyes. "Trace!" she whispered. "I was afraid you liked him, so I didn't want things to be weird, but I'm so glad you don't!"

My breath got stuck somewhere between my sternum and my tonsils. "Oh, yeah. He's all yours." Which was mostly true, but when she said she liked Trace, a flare of jealousy shot through my chest.

Drew shut the locker and started walking down the hall. I fell in stride next to her while the other three girls followed behind us. I felt weird, like I was co-leading a pack of wolves. I could see people watching us, and I felt myself stand a little straighter as we passed through the hall of lockers.

"I just get so nervous around him," Drew said.

I was so disoriented by the fact that I was actually walking down the hall with Drew and her friends that I barely realized that she was talking to me.

"Nervous?" I repeated stupidly. "Around who?"

"Trace!" she said, giving me a *duh* look.

"Oh."

"What should I say to him?" Drew was looking up at me with hopeful eyes, and I couldn't believe that she was actually asking *me* for advice. I kept waiting for someone to jump out of a locker with a video camera and have the whole school yell in unison, "Got ya!"

"Um," I started as I dodged other students coming toward us in the hall, "just say hi to him, I guess."

"Hi." Drew repeated it a couple times in a different voice each time. "Well, this is my next class." I barely got the chance to register what she had said before she disappeared into the classroom. Before I knew it, the other three girls had scattered as well, and I was left standing alone on the opposite side of the school, wondering how I ended up in this place.

chapter thirteen

"*I have no idea why* she wants to be my friend." I was shoveling pretzels into my mouth after school while Jess sat lounging on our couch in the front room. He had been coming inside a lot more since his week and half long stay at our house last Christmas. "I mean, she already has a million friends. Why does she need another one?"

"Maybe she heard about your photography skills and is hoping you'll give her some pointers."

I scowled and tossed a couch pillow at his head.

"You're not allowed to tease me about that yet! It's still too fresh. The wounds haven't completely healed."

Jess threw back his head. His eyes were squeezed shut, and he choked on his breath for a second. "It was a year ago!"

"It's still too fresh," I repeated with a smug look on my face. "I'll let you know when I've healed. Speaking of Trace..." I looked up at Jess from just under my eyelids. "Drew likes him."

Jess's laughter died down, and he focused on my face. "That shouldn't be a big deal. Last I heard, he didn't deserve you."

I looked down at my fingers, which were pulling at a loose string on my sweatshirt. "I guess," I muttered. After a few silent seconds I looked back up at Jess, who was silently watching me with a searching expression.

"Do you still like him?" Jess asked, and I couldn't tell if he was jealous or just confused—or both.

I carefully thought about my response to his question. Yes, I had to admit to at least myself that I still got flustered whenever Trace was present. And that, yes, I still got slightly disoriented whenever he and I made eye contact. But I was also starting to have feelings for Jess. I couldn't explain it to myself, so how was I supposed to explain it to Jess?

"You know what I want to do sometime?" Jess said before I could answer. I knew he was diverting the conversation topic on purpose.

I shook my head. "No, what?"

"I want to go to Niagara Falls."

I wasn't expecting that. "Niagara Falls?" I twisted my face. Of all places to dream about visiting, he chose Niagara Falls?

He ignored my reaction. "Have you ever been to Niagara Falls?" he repeated the name with reverence, as though it were a sacred place.

I scowled. "You know I've never been there, Jess." He knew every place I had ever been. And he knew my vacation history was limited to Cape Cod and one trip to Florida for my great Aunt Lucy's funeral.

"I've wanted to go to Niagara Falls ever since I saw the original Superman movie. You know, the one with Christopher Reeves?"

"Superman?"

"Yeah, you remember. The kid falls off the ledge at Niagara Falls, and Superman saves him."

"That wasn't Niagara Falls." I retorted.

"Of course it was. Where else would it be?"

"Why would Superman go to Niagara Falls?"

"He goes there with Lois Lane."

"I am absolutely positive that you're wrong."

"Either way, I'm going to go there someday." He started twisting a pillow in his hands. "I love water."

I didn't respond. I was too busy trying to flip the battery cover off our television's remote control. Jess sat up abruptly. "Why don't we go to the lake more often?"

Jess and I lived on the shores of Lake Emery. It was just a small fishing lake, and during the summer months it was our home away from home. But during the winter months it was muggy and cold and mostly frozen over.

"Because the lake is boring and gross in the winter," I replied as I snapped the battery cover off with my fingernail.

"Let's go now!" Jess sat up straight and looked at me for an encouraging response.

"What are we going to do at the lake?" I whined. "It's cold."

"Let's just ride our bikes down there and take a look."

I shrugged my shoulders, which Jess took as consent. He flew to his feet and grabbed my hand in one fell swoop as he headed for my front door.

I blew on my hands as we weaved in and out of the trees that separated the main road from the lake. It had been an uncharacteristically warm day for the middle of March, but it was still too cold to ride a bike without gloves. We had parked our bikes by the edge of the road and were now making our way on foot through the mud and dead leaves that were between us and the lake.

"My dad wants partial custody." He kicked through a pile of moldy wood chunks as he spoke.

His announcement came out of nowhere, and even though I was shocked to hear it, it somehow explained his sudden need to go on a random bike ride to the lake in the middle of March.

I pushed a dead branch out of our path. "That can't happen, can it? Not after what he did?"

Jess shrugged and shook his head. "I'm not sure." As he spoke, we both lifted our heads toward the voices coming from the shoreline just twenty feet ahead of us.

"Oh, no." I was disappointed. "There are other people here."

"Good," Jess replied. "I'm glad other people are enjoying this place."

I looked at him in disgust, and then I looked down at my mud-covered blue jeans. I heard the voices more loudly. I cleared one branch away and then another until I saw four girls sitting on the sand at the edge of the pond. Even though I could only see the back of their heads, I knew immediately who they were; Drew, Carmen, Stella, and Stephanie. I wanted to turn around and bolt before they could see me, but a branch snapped under my sneaker and they instantaneously turned around.

"Gemma?" Drew spoke first. She was obviously surprised, but I thought I sensed some annoyance in her voice. Did she think I followed them? Maybe it was in my head. Before I could respond, Jess stepped out of the trees behind me. All four girls stared at him with shocked expressions. I was positive that they were wondering what a guy like him was doing with a girl like me.

"Who's your friend?" Drew nodded toward Jess. The same protection I had felt over my secret non-friendship with Trace earlier that day took over me again now, only ten times stronger.

"Uh," I stammered. I was tempted to give him a fake name like Bruce or A.J. in order to keep him safe from their future conversations.

"I thought you said you didn't have a *boyfriend*." Skepticism dripped from Stephanie's words as she spoke.

I ignored her. "This is Jess Tyler."

Drew's eyes widened as she looked straight past me at Jess and lifted one eyebrow. "Hi, Jess Tyler, it's nice to meet you. I've heard a lot about you."

It was absolutely impossible to find anything wrong with her greeting to Jess. Unlike Clarissa's brash form of flirting, Drew was subtle and cool. I hated it. I had to wonder, though, where she had heard about Jess. I had never told her about him.

Jess shifted behind me. "Do you girls go to school with Gem?"

"Gem?" Drew sat up straighter and looked at me with a devious smile. "I like that."

I looked down at the dirt and mumbled, "Don't call me Gem."

Jess patted me on the back. "She thinks it sounds too much like Jim."

Jess loved calling me Gem, despite the fact that I had begged him not to for years. It didn't bother me anymore when he said it, though. It was like a little pet name he had for me. But I still cringed whenever anyone else said it. And for some reason it was driving me twice as crazy to hear it from Drew.

"I think it's cute," Drew said while smiling at Jess.

I turned to Jess and reluctantly told him their names. I spoke in a steady tone, but my eyes pleaded with him not to give away the fact that I had been talking about them all afternoon. Jess read my cue and nonchalantly walked toward the shore line of the pond. "It's nice to meet you all." He picked up a couple pebbles and tossed them into the pond. All four girls had their eyes glued to the back of his head. I could have painted a picture of them in the length of time they spent watching him. I looked at the back of Jess to see what was so incredible that all four of them would be watching him with drool practically dripping down their chins. Okay, I knew Jess was tall and good looking. But there were a lot of good-looking guys in Franklin. Why was Jess getting so much attention from some of the most popular girls in town? He had on a Philly's hat that he wore backward on his head, his brown hair curled softly out the ends and around his ears. He was wearing a midnight blue hooded sweatshirt with the sleeves pushed up around his forearms so that they wouldn't get dirty as he picked up rocks. He wore a pair of old Lucky Brand jeans which, now that I looked at them, fell over his lower half perfectly. And to finish it off he was wearing some old running shoes that were now soaked in mud and dead leaves.

"You can skip rocks," Drew spoke lowly and evenly as she boosted herself from the ground and shook off the sand that was stuck to her jeans. She walked toward Jess, who was launching his third stone into the pond. It skipped over the water four times then disappeared beneath the black surface.

Jess squinted into the sun. "Not really. I think that last one was a record for me."

Drew stepped so close to him that they were nearly touching. She looked so tiny next to him. She picked up a semi-flat stone and tossed it effortlessly across the glassy water. It skipped at least six times before it disappeared.

Jess looked sincerely amazed. "Impressive." He nodded as he watched the pond, looking to see if her stone was still skipping. "Where did you learn to do that?"

I felt angry that the other girls and I were all silently watching their interaction. It was like Drew and Jess were the main characters of a movie, and we were all watching and waiting for them to fall in love and live happily ever after.

I quietly walked over to where the other girls were still sitting and plopped myself on the dirt next to Stella. "Do you guys come here a lot?" I was trying as hard as I could to not be bothered by the skipping rock conversation going on ten feet away from me.

Not one of the three girls looked at me. They kept their gaze toward Drew and Jess. Stella finally shrugged her shoulders. "We do lately. There's not much more to do around here."

Stephanie chimed in next, "I can't wait until I graduate so I can get out of this lame town."

I looked out over the lake and down the shore line. Even though the beauty of the lake had been lost in the past five months of snow and ice, it still held a million memories for me of past summers with Jess. Directly across the lake was the dock where Jess taught me how to fish. That summer I caught a fish so big that it took both of us to reel it in. Down the shore a ways from where we were sitting was the old rope swing that we'd hung a few years before. And just beyond the rope swing was the boat dock. One of our favorite things to do was to go down there on summer nights with any other kids we could convince to go with us and play hide-and-go-seek on all the old fishing boats. Nothing got my heart beating faster than hiding all alone in the bow of an old fishing boat at night on the quiet lake, waiting for someone to find me. I loved this lake—even in March—and I loved this town. And unlike Stephanie, I never wanted to leave.

My attention drifted back to Drew and Jess. I couldn't hear what they were saying, but they were both laughing and apparently having a good time together. Drew reached over and touched Jess's elbow. It looked like she was telling him to keep it close to his ribs in order to skip the rocks better. But something nasty, hard, and cold swelled in my stomach as I watched her hold on to his elbow and then his forearm. And then as if it couldn't get any worse, he smiled at her. It wasn't just a smile to be polite. It was the Jess smile. The Jess smile that belonged to me.

Without giving myself time to consider the consequences, I got up from the dirt, removed my Nike tennis shoes, dug my toes into the sand, and then set off running toward the water. I ran as fast as I could and finished with a cannon ball into the ice cold liquid. I was so shocked with what I had just done that the temperature of the water didn't register to my brain. All I could feel was the slushy mud under my feet as my head sank beneath the water. All at once I felt a million tiny jabs of ice pierce every inch of my body. My head throbbed as the water swirled around it, jabbing at my eyes and inner ears. The pond was quite shallow so my head bobbed back up within a couple seconds, but even though my mouth was well out of the water again, I couldn't catch my breath. I opened my eyes, though I could barely make out the figures standing on the shore in front of me. I blinked the water away from my eyelashes and was finally able to gasp on a breath of air.

I heard Jess's voice. "Gemma! Are you crazy?" His voice was strained as he side-stepped along the water line to get closer to me. All the girls were quiet, though as I continued to blink I could tell that they were watching with wild excitement, especially Drew. Jess looked terrified as he began pushing his way toward me through the knee-deep water. I tried standing up as the water must have only been four feet deep where I was, but the mud underneath me was too loose, and I couldn't get my footing. I tried swimming toward Jess, but my arms and legs were too cold. I could barely feel them attached to my body. They felt more like blocks of ice attached to me with staples rather than arms and legs. The girls on the beach began shrieking with terror as they realized that I was drifting further away. Before I knew what was happening, Jess was at my side, chest-deep in the water.

"Here, take my hand." He reached for me, and I tried to reach back, but my arm felt like it weighed a hundred pounds.

"I don't think I can," I spoke quickly. I was starting to panic. My body had never felt immovable like this. All I could do was cock my head back to keep my face out of the water, but my feet were sinking into the mud, and it was getting harder and harder to stay above the waves.

Jess moved quickly toward me until the water was up to his chin. "Grab my hand, Gemma." He reached out as far as he could, but the water was lapping me away from shore, and his fingertips were still six inches away from my bobbing body.

"I'm freezing Jess. I can't move my—" I couldn't even finish my sentence. A piece of my hair fell against my cheek. It felt stiff and cold like an ice cycle.

"Gemma!" Panic screamed from Jess's eyes as he dove toward me. He was completely buried in the icy-cold liquid. And within seconds I felt him wrap both of his arms firmly around my waist. His grip felt like thorns against my body as he dragged me to the shore that was a mere ten feet in front of us. I felt so helpless. I couldn't move any part of my body, and yet somehow every part of me was shaking uncontrollably. Jess dragged me to the dry sand, and Drew handed him his sweatshirt, which he had quickly discarded before jumping in the water. He wrapped it around my shoulders, but it only pressed my icy clothes closer to my skin. Drew handed her jacket to Jess next.

"Will this help?" Her expression was eager and sincere.

Jess was breathing hard. He must have been freezing himself. "Yes, but not with all these wet clothes on her. I'm going to go to the road and flag someone down to help us. You need to take off her wet clothes and cover her up with the dry jackets."

The next thing I knew Jess was gone and the four girls were hovering over me, carefully taking off my soaking sweatshirt and jeans. I was embarrassed but relieved to have the heavy clothes that might as well have been sheets of ice removed from my body. One of the girls draped Jess's jacket over my shoulders and zipped it up, while another girl fashioned a sort of skirt for me with Drew's jacket. I felt another dry jacket wrapped around my head and two others swaddling my feet and lower legs. I felt like a mummy, but it was a hundred times better. I heard Jess's voice before I had realized he had returned.

"Good job. She's already looking better." I felt tired, and though not quite so icy, I still felt cold. I dreamed of being home in front of the fireplace drinking hot chocolate. Again I felt Jess's grip—this time under my shoulder blades and my knees as he carried me away from the lake and through the trees. Jess loaded me into the backseat of a car. I recognized the man and woman in the front seat as the Bartons, an older couple that lived on our street. I heard Jess and the four girls saying something outside, and then Jess slipped onto the backseat next to me and held me close to him as the car made its way down the road. He rubbed my arm with his hand so vigorously I thought the jacket might start on fire. Shame overwhelmed me as I thought about myself jumping into the freezing cold lake at free will. This whole catastrophe would have been a completely different situation, almost romantic, had I been thrust into the pond by an unexpected gust of wind. But the fact that I jumped in made me feel like an idiot. Maybe I was remembering it wrong. I was probably in shock and thinking incorrectly. Maybe I hadn't jumped in after all! When my lips felt thawed enough to move, I said in a frail whisper, "What happened?"

Jess looked down at the top of my head that was nuzzled into his chest. "You jumped into the water," he replied callously.

I *had* jumped into the water, and Jess was upset about it, as he rightfully should be. "Why?" I felt so tired and weak. I meant for the question to be rhetorical. I didn't expect Jess to know the answer, but he sighed and said, "I could make a guess."

I found the strength to sit up and look at him for his guess.

But his head was turned away from me as he stared out the window.

"Can I ask you another question?" I was beginning to feel warm again, but I stayed close to Jess partly to offer him my heat, and mostly because I loved being near him.

He looked down at me again and nodded his head.

"You don't really think you're dad will be able to get partial custody, do you?"

Jess looked out the window, and I felt him breathe heavier underneath me. "I don't know." And then he said the last thing I ever thought I'd hear him say. "I feel sorry for him."

I was so surprised with his answer that I didn't have a

response. All I could do was lean against his chest and hold him. And hope that I never had to let go.

We didn't speak another word before the Bartons pulled into my driveway. I mumbled a thank you and a good-bye as Jess gently dragged me off their backseat, but the good-bye was unnecessary because they anxiously followed us up my front walk and even through my front door. Mr. Barton had called my parents from his cell phone, so they were expecting us with the fire lit and an electric blanket draped over the couch. Jess explained my clothing situation to my mom, who led me up the stairs to the bathroom to take off the rest of my wet underclothes.

"Where's Jess?" My skin had thawed out considerably and talking came much easier as Mom led me back down the stairs twenty minutes later in a dry set of pajamas. Dad was sitting on the couch opposite of the one set up for me, reading the newspaper. As soon as he heard my voice, he jumped to his feet and led me from the staircase to the couch, where he helped me lie down. Physically, I probably didn't need all this help, but emotionally I was drained, so I accepted it easily. Once I was lying on the couch, Dad draped the electric blanket over me while Mom laid a bag of warm rice on my head. The warmth of the blanket, the fire, and the rice bag enveloped me. This was exactly what I had been dreaming about when I was drenched in ice. The smell of the rice filled my nostrils, and I closed my eyes and listened to the popping of the fire.

"Where did Jess go?" I repeated. No one had answered my question.

"He went home," Dad said.

That made sense. I didn't know why he would have stayed.

"Is it true that you did a cannonball into Lake Emery?" Dad

asked. He watched me with narrowed eyes, hoping that he had heard wrong, that there was actually a much better explanation.

I folded my arms over my face, which Dad would know was an indicator that—yes, it was true, and yes, I did feel really dumb for doing it.

"What in the world, Gemma?" Mom said as she sat down by my feet and rubbed my legs. "You could have been seriously hurt. *Jess* could have been seriously hurt. You are lucky things turned out as well as they did."

I opened my eyes slightly and made the most pained expression I could muster. "I have no idea what I was thinking. It just happened!"

"What were you doing at the lake this time of year anyway?" Dad asked.

I told them the whole story from Jess's love for Niagara Falls to Drew touching Jess's elbow. "Drew was throwing herself all over him. It was disgusting!"

Dad looked unconvinced. "So you jumped into a freezing lake?"

"No, it wasn't because of that."

Mom chuckled under her breath.

I looked at her quizzically. "You think I jumped because she was flirting with Jess?"

"I think you were upset because Jess wasn't giving you his one hundred percent attention. And I think you thought he would start paying attention to you again if you did something a bit outlandish."

I pulled the blanket up over my chin and sank behind it. The last thing I wanted to be was one of those girls that did lame things for attention. But that's exactly what I had done.

"The ironic thing about it," Dad added without looking up from his newspaper, "is that you're the last girl on earth that would need to go the extra mile to get the attention of Jess Tyler."

chapter fourteen

"*I can't believe you never* told me you were friends with Jess Tyler." Drew and I had decided to be partners on an assignment in German class the next day, much to the chagrin of the three other girls, who didn't even try to hide their distaste for my presence in their group. Unfortunately, my episode at the lake hadn't so much as given me the sniffles, so I had no excuse to stay home from school. Unlike Jess, who could barely get out of bed that morning. I wasn't too upset about going to school, though. Now that I actually had locker partners and someone to walk down the halls with, school wasn't all that bad.

I pulled a red-colored pencil out of the color box as I replied, "I didn't know you knew who he was. I didn't think it would matter."

"Of course I know who he is." Drew bit her lip as she scribbled on the paper in front of us. "Everyone knows who Jess Tyler is. I had just never met him before."

"How do you know who he is?" I was waiting for her to further prove my point that Jess was indeed popular.

Drew shrugged. "Girls talk. And my brother goes to school with him, so I hear things. He just has one of those names."

I nodded my head, even though I didn't entirely know what she meant by that.

"Gemma," Drew asked while dropping her colored pencil back into the box, "who gave you that bracelet?"

I looked at the bracelet. It was on my right hand, and so it dangled as I scribbled over the page with the colored pencil.

"I told you, it was a Christmas present," I replied.

"Right, from a friend," she said smugly. "Did Jess give it to you?"

"Yes." I shrugged my shoulders like it wasn't a big deal.

She stopped coloring instantly and looked straight at my face. "What is up with you two? Are you a couple or something?"

It was killing her not to know, and there was a part of me that wished I could have smashed her hopes entirely and told her, "Yes! We are a couple, actually, so stay away!" But we weren't, so I couldn't. And so I said, "No. We're just friends."

She paused for a minute, just watching me scribble before picking out a new colored pencil from the box. She turned back to her own scribbling then said, "I don't get you, Gemma Mitchell."

"So according to Drew, you have 'one of those names.'"

Jess sneezed and wiped his nose with a tissue. He was lying in bed still, but he was well enough by the afternoon to see visitors—or at least to see me. "What is that supposed to mean?"

"It means that everyone talks about you, everyone knows you, and everyone likes you."

Jess sniffed again and let out a horse sounding laugh. "What, Drew knows two people who know who I am, and suddenly I'm a household name?"

"You're popular. And you can't deny it."

Jess ignored me and steered the conversation another way. "How's the situation with Drew and Trace? Have you given her any killer advice yet of how to get him to notice her?" Jess relaxed into his pillow and then added, "How do you get yourself into these situations?"

"I don't think I have to worry about Trace anymore." I pulled on the rubber of my sole, and it finally snapped off. "I think she has a new crush." I looked at Jess, who still looked pale and clammy. "You." I waited for Jess's response, nervous that he would be happy to know that Drew liked him.

Jess scrunched his face. "Perfect. Is there a dance coming up soon? You could talk her into asking me to waltz."

I threw a pillow at Jess's face. "I thought I was doing you a favor."

Jess laughed behind the pillow, and then his laugh turned into a series of raspy coughs.

"I'm sorry you're sick," I said guiltily. "I'm the one that should be sick."

"I'm just glad you're not at the bottom of the lake," he said with a serious tone when he caught his breath.

"Yeah, that was pretty dumb of me."

"Just promise me one thing." Jess patted my knee as he closed his eyes and held onto his head with the other hand.

His touch sent a million flutters up my spine. I looked at him, waiting for the one thing I was silently promising.

"Next time you want my attention, don't try to kill yourself. I kind of like having you around."

"When's your birthday, Gem?"

I had just dropped my biology book on top of Drew's English literature book when she asked. I still wasn't used to hearing the name she had taken to calling me ever since the lake incident. "September seventh," I answered.

"Hmmm. That's no good." Drew was leaning her back against the wall next to her locker while I rummaged through my bag, trying to find my geography packet. Carmen still shared the locker with us, but Stella and Stephanie hardly came around anymore. They had decided to go on strike from being Drew's friend until she appreciated them more. Drew seemed to hardly notice their absence. Carmen showed up at the locker a few seconds later. She had eased up around me since the other two girls weren't around anymore. I guessed she figured it was easier to share Drew with one other girl rather than two.

"Carmen, when's your birthday?"

Carmen stood up straight and looked Drew in the eye. It was apparent that she was hurt. "November third," she spoke quietly but defiantly. I had a feeling that Drew hadn't done anything for her birthday. Drew didn't seem fazed by it.

"That won't work either."

I found the packet and stepped away from the locker so that Carmen could do what she needed to.

"We need to have a party." Drew was still leaning against the wall. Her arms were folded, and she was looking at the blank brick wall across from us. I tucked my book in my backpack and zipped it up.

"Gemma, your parents are going to be out of town all weekend. We would be stupid if we didn't take this chance to have a party."

My stomach turned over inside of me. I should never have mentioned that my parents were going to Florida for a convention for my dad's work.

Drew clapped her hands together. "You know what is even better than a birthday party?" She had bounced away from the wall now and was staring excitedly at Carmen and me. Carmen raised an eyebrow at me as we both waited for the answer. "A *fake* birthday party!"

"Fake birthday?" I more mouthed it than said it.

"Yes! It will be an experiment. Each of us will tell one person that its Gemma's birthday and that we're having a party at her house tonight. We'll see how many people show up!"

Drew's idea ran through my head. My parents had never left Bridget and me home alone overnight before, and I knew they were going to be strict about rules. I figured I could probably talk them into letting me have a couple friends over, but not a whole party. But, then again, nobody else knew who I was anyway. Who would actually go to a birthday party of someone they didn't know?

"I don't think anyone will come, but I guess you can invite one person." I looked at her sharply in the eye and held one finger in front of her face. "Just one person."

Drew beamed. "We *each* will invite one person, and I think your one person should be Jess."

This aggravated me, but I pretended not to care. "No, Jess isn't into parties. Especially fake ones."

Drew raised her eyebrows in surprise. "Jess Tyler? Not into parties? I don't buy it."

"It's true." I flung my backpack over my shoulder and pulled a piece of gum out of my pocket.

Drew narrowed her eyes. "You know who he hangs out with, right?"

"Yeah, me." I unwrapped the gum and folded it into my mouth. I had to chew with my mouth open to fit it all in.

"I mean at school and on the weekends." Drew watched me carefully.

"What are you talking about?"

"He's a partier." Carmen chimed in. I looked at her satisfied expression then at Drew, who had confirming eyes.

"What do you mean? Like with girls and alcohol?"

Drew nodded with one eyebrow raised. "I don't think you know Jess Tyler as well as you think you do."

I was positive they were wrong. Jess and I told each other everything. Besides, I had been in junior high long enough to know how rumors were started and blown up. "You're wrong," I said. "He's not like that."

Drew and Carmen glanced at each other skeptically. "It's not just a stupid rumor, Gemma."

There was no way it could be true. Right? I mean, Jess was always with me. Well, not *always*. I chomped harder on my gum. My jaw was starting to hurt.

Drew raised her eyebrows and sighed as she lifted her backpack off the floor. The bell rang. I was late for class. But I was always late for class these days.

"Invite Trace Weston, then." Drew had changed the topic of conversation as we headed to our classes. I couldn't even remember what we had been talking about before.

"Invite him to what?"

"Your birthday party!"

I remembered the fake birthday as she slipped into her fifth-period classroom. And I was suddenly left standing alone again in the hall, questioning everything I knew.

Drew and Carmen sat quietly on the leather couch in my front room. Carmen was flipping nervously through the *Guinness Book of World Records* that was set out on our coffee table, while Drew twirled her chewed bubble gum around her finger, peering at the book from time to time over Carmen's shoulder. My parents had left a list of chores on the kitchen counter, which I scanned briefly before taking the girls the cups of fruit punch I had offered them a few minutes earlier.

"I'm telling you, no one is going to come," I said as I handed them their drinks. Even though Carmen was always around, I constantly felt like I was solely talking to Drew.

"So what if they don't? We'll just play Pictionary without them." Drew seemed genuinely okay with the idea. I just couldn't figure her out. "Who did you invite anyway?" she asked as an afterthought while chomping on her hardened gum.

"Uh," I stalled by taking a big drink of punch, but I was saved by the ringing of the doorbell. My stomach did a summersault as I jumped to my feet. "Someone's here!" I whispered.

Drew was beaming. "Awesome!" For some reason she whispered too.

"Who did *you* invite?" I shot Drew a panicked look. Bridget was upstairs in her room reading. What would she do? The second I let one more person into our house I was violating my parents' rules. They had specifically told me that I could have no more than two friends over. I really hadn't thought that anyone else would show up!

"I just told Stella," Carmen whispered as she twisted her punch glass in her hand.

"I just told my brother," Drew whispered innocently.

"Your brother?" I screamed, still using my whisper voice. "Isn't he in high school?"

Drew chuckled. "Yeah."

My hand shook as I placed my punch cup on the coffee table. I stood up from the couch and smoothed out my jeans and my new purple v-neck sweater. I walked eagerly toward the front door. I held my breath as I turned the knob and pulled. By the time I got the door open, I felt like I was in the middle of a bad dream. I didn't even recognize my front porch or the seven tall guys standing on it, waiting to come into my house. Not one of them looked slightly familiar. The two guys standing closest to me looked as confused as I was.

"Uh," the biggest one started, "is Drew Markoviak here?"

I became aware that my mouth was wide open with shock. I found the strength to nod my head once and stand back so they could come into my house.

"Hey, guys!" Drew acted so calm. "Come in!" She looked at me hesitantly as I stood holding the front door with horror written on my face. "Guys, this is Gemma." She pointed to me from across the room. "It's her birthday today." Lie. "She's turning sixteen." Bigger lie. I finally gained the sense of mind to start closing the door when I heard another group of people coming up our walkway. I squinted into the dark and counted at least ten people—boys and girls this time—headed toward the front door. They all filed past me into my house. One girl handed me an unopened bottle of designer lotion with a bow tied around it. It took me a second to realize that it was a birthday present. I set it on a table next to the door and walked into the front room where everyone was gathering. Someone had turned on the radio that was above our television set, and a couple girls had found the punch in the kitchen and were bringing cups of it to everyone in the room. A moving body caught the corner of my eye, and I looked up toward the staircase where Bridget was standing in total shock.

"Gemma!" she mouthed as she waved me over to her with her hand.

I quickly weaved in and out of the people in the room and those who were still filing in—at least three other groups had shown up—until I reached the staircase.

"Are you insane?" she yelled at me over the music that was now blaring from the living room. "Mom and Dad are going to kill you!"

"I had no idea! I didn't think this many people would come! Please don't call Mom and Dad. Please!"

Bridget looked over my head at the twenty to thirty kids filling our living room and kitchen. "Okay, but if they find out, we're both going to get in trouble, and then you'll be doing my chores for the rest of the year."

Bridget wanted to be a lawyer some day, and she was already an expert at making deals.

"All of your chores?"

Bridget gave me a threatening look.

"Fine!" I whispered and turned to go back downstairs. I was standing on the bottom step, scanning the crowd when the same big guy who had asked about Drew Markoviak yelled over all the noise of the house with a big voice.

"Listen up, everyone!" A couple people made shushing sounds with their teeth and soon the room was quiet. The big guy continued, "Okay, listen up! It's Gemma's birthday today, and she's turning the big one-six!" Thirty heads looked around trying to find this "Gemma" that the big guy was talking about. I knew that none of them knew who I was. "And I've been told that Gemma has been waiting for her sixteenth birthday to have her first kiss." He continued as the room filled with hushed laughter. "So, I was hoping that the birthday girl might accept my request to be her very first kiss." Everyone in the room broke into cheering and clapping. A few guys were howling and whistling and patting the guy on the back. I saw Drew's face in the crowd. She was looking at me from the corner of her eye while holding a cup of punch up to her lips and smiling. Someone over by the stereo yelled, "Who's Gemma?" And someone by the door yelled, "I think this is her house." Someone else in the kitchen yelled, "I think she left." Again I heard some shushing sounds, the main one coming from the big guy doing the talking. "Please! Please be quiet! Gemma's the beautiful sixteen-year-old on the stairs. This is her house, and it's her birthday. Show some respect." I couldn't tell if he was mocking me. He didn't sound entirely sincere. But he continued, "Now please be quiet. I need an answer from the birthday girl." The room was dead quiet again. Everyone in the room watched me with anxious eyes. I had read in a lot of books the description of someone's knees going weak when they felt nervous, but I had never quite understood the reality of the feeling until that moment.

"Uh." My voice was shaking, and sweat was building up in my armpits. I tucked some hair behind my ear. "I don't even know you."

"Oh! I apologize!" The big kid set down his own cup of punch on the coffee table and weaved in and out of people until he reached me at the bottom of the stairs. I was standing a step above him, but he was still as tall as I was. He stuck his large, tan hand toward me, and with a big, white-toothed smile he introduced himself, "I'm Greg Markoviak."

Markoviak? Was this Drew's *brother*? I had always pictured anyone in Drew's family to be smaller. He had black hair just like Drew, but other than that they didn't look a thing like each other. He had a dark tan complexion and silvery gray eyes. His pearly white, perfectly straight teeth took up half of his face. He had a profound nose that only someone as good looking as him could pull off. I looked across the room to Drew and found her watching me with curious eyes. Another big handsome high-school kid had his arm draped around her shoulders. I realized that the room was still quiet, and everyone was waiting for my response. I lightly grasped Greg's outreached hand in mine. "It's nice to meet you."

"Tell you what." I assumed Greg was still talking to me, but he turned around so that everyone in the room—and the house for that matter—could hear what he was saying. "I'll make you a deal, Gemma. I have a quarter here in my pocket." Greg started digging through every pocket in his jeans. After a couple awkward seconds, a boy who was leaning on the doorframe leading to the kitchen stepped forward and offered Greg a quarter. "Thanks, Tim," Greg said as he took the quarter. "Gemma." He turned back to me. "Here's the deal." He held the quarter above his head so everyone could see it. "I bet you this quarter that I can kiss you *without* touching you." There was a laugh from somewhere near the television. Greg hushed the laugh and continued, "No really, I think it's possible. I think I can kiss Gemma here without even touching her." Greg turned around so that he was facing me again. "So the deal is, Gemma, that if I can kiss you without touching you, then I get to keep the quarter. But if I can't, then I'll give the quarter to you." My head was spinning with confusion, embarrassment, and fear. First of all, I couldn't figure out what he was even talking about? Kiss me without touching me? Was that even possible? I didn't know much about kissing, but I thought the main gist of it was the *touching* part. And second of all, what if he did kiss me? In front of all of these people? I had been waiting for my first kiss all my life. I had pictured it being a lot more romantic than this. And preferably with someone I had known longer than ten seconds! I looked at all the exits in the room. The front door as well as the hall to the kitchen were both blocked by wide-eyed spectators. The only way was up the stairs. Then I caught a glimpse of Drew from the corner of my eye. All of her friends were here. And the guy standing in front of me was her brother! I couldn't bolt now. At least thirty pairs of eyes were watching me in silence, waiting for me to answer.

I swallowed hard. "Okay." I couldn't believe the word had come out of my mouth. But I had said it, and before I could change my mind Greg yelled, "So it's a deal!" He reached his hand out to me once again to finalize the deal. I lightly grasped his hand and nodded.

"Deal."

The room around us was hushed. It seemed as though no one even dared to breathe, including myself. Greg's toothy smile faded away as his expression turned more serious. His gaze went from my eyes to my mouth, and I could feel him leaning in closer to me. In fact, it felt like everyone in the room leaned a little closer at that moment. Thoughts of doubt and uncertainty filled my mind. What was happening? Was he going to kiss me? Was he not? And what if he did? I had always dreamed of my first kiss being with someone I truly liked, someone like Jess. And in a romantic place, like under a waterfall at sunset. Not in my living room, with a guy I just met, and in front of a bunch of strangers. Greg was inching closer, and I could feel his breath on my cheek. My stomach flipped over inside itself, and I felt an overwhelming wave of nausea. What if he did kiss me? I had no idea how to kiss! What if I messed up? I didn't even know how to move my lips? What if we bumped noses? His nose was so big! How was I supposed to dodge it in order to get to his mouth? And if I got there, what was I supposed to do next? Should I pucker? Should I have my lips slightly parted like they do it in the movies? What if he used his tongue? What if he tasted gross? What if *I* tasted gross?

Greg's lips were only millimeters away from mine. My face tensed up as I squeezed my eyes shut and pursed my lips in a tight, awkward pucker. In the final second before Greg's lips touched mine, the front door hinge made a high, squeaky sound that caught the attention of everyone in the room, especially Greg and me. I looked up and over Greg's big head to see that standing in the doorway with an expression of horror worse than my own, was Jess.

chapter fifteen

Jess was panting and out of breath. His face was red, and it was apparent that he had sprinted here from his house. He looked at me in total shock then slammed the door behind him. "What's going on here, Gemma?"

I was stunned silent. I couldn't have said a word even if I had something to say, which I didn't.

Jess continued, "Why are these people here?" He waved his hand around the room, never taking his eyes off of me.

"Dude, Jess," Greg piped in. He was still holding my hand in his. "It's just a party. There's no reason to be so upset about it."

Jess's gaze turned to Greg, his eyes blistering with anger. "*Just* a party, Greg? And I'm sure that red liquid in your cup is *just* fruit punch."

Greg let go of my hand and looked down at the cup he was holding.

"It *is* fruit punch, Jess," I spoke for the first time since Jess entered the scene. "What else would it be?"

Greg looked at me with big eyes like a puppy that had just made an accident on the carpet.

Jess ignored my question, but his attention was now turned to me. "Were you actually going to kiss him?"

I moved my lips, searching for the best explanation, but I was too embarrassed to tell him the truth.

Jess turned his head back to Greg. "Do you know how old she is?" Jess stepped closer to Greg. I was surprised that they were the same height.

"She's sixteen. Today is her birthday." Greg's voice sounded strange when he wasn't yelling above a noisy crowd.

"She goes to school with your little sister. You really think she's sixteen?"

Jess was angry, and everyone in the room felt his fury. There wasn't a face in the crowd that wasn't listening intently to what he was saying. Greg was stunned. For the first time that night, he didn't have anything to say.

"She's fifteen!" Jess spat it out of his mouth as if he were calling me a whore or an adulterer. Greg looked quickly at me then down at his cup. Jess waited for a response, but when none was given, he turned to the rest of the crowd. "Everyone, out!" There wasn't too much more that could shock me after the events that had taken place that night. But I was floored with everyone's reaction to Jess's command. Everybody in the room scattered toward the door with hardly a word. The house was empty within seconds. I hadn't moved from my place on the step, and Jess was still standing in the same place as well. Drew had moved toward the door but stayed standing just inside it, holding onto her coat. Bridget had come out of her room upstairs and was watching us all from over the banister. The vaulted ceilings over the front room allowed her to have a bird's eye view of everything that was going on. I wished so badly that I was up where she was instead of down here.

Jess's anger filled face expression softened slightly. "Are you okay, Gem?"

I nodded slowly, biting my bottom lip in an effort not to cry.

"What happened? Why were all those people here? Do you even know any of them?"

Jess's assumption—no matter how true it was—that I wouldn't know who any of those "popular" people were jabbed at the core of my chest. I was so angry at him for barging in and making me look like a fool in front of all those people. I stormed down the bottom step, past Jess, and into the kitchen, where I started angrily empty-ing the clean dishes out of our dishwasher. Jess followed me into the kitchen. "Gem, I don't know what's going on, but you really put yourself into a dangerous situation here."

I banged the pots and pans together loudly as I inserted a clean pot into the cupboard.

"There was alcohol in those cups, Gemma. Alcohol! Every person in here was underage. And *you* are *way* underage!"

My chest heaved with anger as I practically chucked all the clean Tupperware into the rotisserie. Jess had walked around the counter and was standing right next to the dishwasher, so I had to dodge him every time I turned to put something away. For a moment I wondered about Drew and Bridget but figured— if they were still around—that they had intelligently decided to stay out of the fight.

"And the image of you and Greg—almost kissing!" Jess grabbed his head as if he had a terrible headache. "I'll never be able to get that image out of my mind! Seriously, Gemma, were you really going to *kiss* him?"

I was emptying the utensil tray now, not even paying attention to making sure each utensil got in its correct slot. I couldn't look Jess in the eye. I had never felt such anger and resentment toward him—or anybody for that matter—in my whole life.

"How did all those people get here anyway? Did you actually invite them?"

"That's it!" I yelled while slamming a plastic pitcher on the counter in front of me. "You have absolutely no right to be saying those things!"

Jess looked shocked, but I didn't care.

"You say I shouldn't hang out with those people? You say I shouldn't have alcohol at my parties! But tell me this, Jess, how did Greg Markoviak–someone who is obviously a partier–know who you are?" I slammed the empty dishwasher door closed and folded my arms across my chest.

Jess's tone was cautious and slow. "What are you talking about?"

My tone was opposite, hyper and fast. "Drew said that you're a partier. That you hang out with people that drink and do all sorts of bad stuff." I relaxed my arms and took a deep breath. "I didn't believe her at first, but now I don't know what to think!" I could feel the cruelty in my voice. I had never dreamed of speaking to Jess this way. I had never dreamed of feeling such animosity toward him.

"You believe Drew?" His words were soft and even.

"Yes."

"The same Drew who invited her brother and all of his *drunk* friends over here to take advantage of you?"

I felt defensive, for Drew or myself, I wasn't sure. "That's not true." Or was it?

"The same Drew who told everyone it was your sixteenth birthday?"

I was stunned silent.

"Yeah, I can see how you would trust *Drew*. She's proven herself to be a truly loyal friend." His words were drenched in sarcasm.

"Why would she lie about you being a partier?"

"How would I be at parties on the weekends when I'm always here, with *you?*" Jess suddenly looked tired. He brushed his fingers through his hair, but he was still looking at me in the eyes. "If you can't trust the person you've been friends with for most your life, what makes you suddenly so keen on trusting a girl you've known for a month?"

I didn't have an answer for him. I stood in front of him, holding onto the dishwasher handle, feeling unsure about everything. My house had never sounded so quiet. It was a shameful silence.

"I should go." He sounded serious but not angry.

"Why didn't you tell me that you knew who she was?" I asked angrily as a last attempt to win the conversation.

"Who?" He cringed with exhaustion.

"You knew that Greg was Drew's brother, so you must have known when I was talking about her for the past couple months who she was. Why didn't you warn me? Why didn't you tell me the Markoviaks are trouble?"

Jess sadly lifted his shoulders then dropped them in defeat. "I don't know. I guess I wanted to let you figure things out for yourself."

I let both of my arms flop in the air and slap against my sides. "Well that would be a *first!*"

Jess shook his head and turned to walk out of the kitchen. He had almost disappeared behind the wall that led to the front door when he turned and looked at me. "I'm always *here*, Gemma." Jess's eyes were glued to mine. "With *you*."

I swallowed hard as I felt the salt of tears filling the crevices behind my eyes. I watched him step out of sight. I listened to him close the front door as he left. Then I allowed the tears to flow down my cheeks.

chapter sixteen

My parents got home late the next afternoon from their trip. They both smelled like an airport terminal as they breezed happily from the garage into the kitchen, where Bridget and I were both making dinner. We thought it would be a good idea to kiss up to them as much as possible in case one of the neighbors mentioned the number of strange cars outside our house the night before.

Bridget was a beautiful faker. She lied perfectly when my parents asked her how everything went while they were gone.

"Fine." She yawned. "Not much happened. It was kind of boring, actually."

My parents bought it easily. After all, why should they have any reason to doubt? Neither one of their daughters had done so much as stayed out past curfew since we were old enough to have a curfew. We were basically the easiest kids a parent could ask for, most of the time.

All through dinner my parents gabbed about their trip. Dad had a meeting the first morning for work, and after that he had a vacation with my mom all paid for by his company. Mom's eyes were as big as baseballs as she whipped out gift after gift for Bridget and me that they had bought at the hotel and museums they'd gone to.

The more happy and easygoing my parents were, the more guilt-ridden and panicked I became. Bridget didn't seem to be fazed by the fact that we had blatantly lied to our parents. I, on the other hand, felt like the whole earth was spinning off its axis because of it. I stayed strong as long as I could, convincing myself that it was better for everyone in my family if my parents just never knew about it. It could be one of those funny stories I finally confessed about fifteen years down the road when I was safely married with three kids. We would all have a big laugh about it then.

But I did a terrible job convincing myself. I nearly vomited every time I was around my parents for the rest of the night, especially if either one of them looked me in the eye. It was nearly ten o'clock, and my parents were in their bedroom getting ready for bed. My dad had a toothbrush jammed halfway down his throat—he was a huge advocate of brushing until your gums bled—and my mom was sitting on the bed in her pajamas, flipping through an old *Home Journal* magazine. On any normal night at this time, I would breeze by their bedroom yelling a "goodnight and I love you," but tonight wasn't a normal night. Nothing about my life was normal so long as this lie was swirling around my head.

I stepped cautiously into their bedroom. "Hey!"

Mom looked up from her magazine. "Hi, honey." She looked back down and licked her finger to turn the page.

"So it sounds like you guys had a good trip," I said for the millionth time that night. We had been doing nothing but talking about their trip all evening.

Mom looked up at me with tired but kind eyes. I could hear my dad spitting toothpaste into the sink in their master bathroom. "Yes, we did. And everything was all right here?" I wasn't sure if she meant to make it sound like a question, but I felt like I needed to give her an answer.

I felt my palms starting to sweat, and I began swaying back and forth from the balls of my feet to my heels. "I actually need to talk to you guys about that."

Dad's attention was caught, and he walked into the bedroom, water still dripping from his chin.

"About what?" Mom closed her magazine and set it on the nightstand. I had their undivided attention, and suddenly I was scared to death.

"Remember how you told me I could have two friends over last night?"

They both watched me carefully, not saying a word.

"Well, for about a half hour there were more like thirty people here."

Both of their eyes bulged out from their eyelids. "Thirty people? Here?" My mom squinted her eyes at me as though she was having a hard time seeing.

I grimaced and nodded my head. "Drew thought it would be fun to have a fake birthday party for me."

"A fake birthday?" Mom asked. She actually sounded calm.

"Who's Drew?" Dad asked.

"It's Gemma's new friend at school," Mom answered him, but she was still staring at me.

"Yeah, she wanted to have a birthday party, but none of us have birthdays in March, so she wanted to see how many people would come here if we told them it was my birthday."

Both of my parents rolled their eyes.

"I know, I know," I continued. "In hindsight it seems totally obvious that a whole bunch of people would show up because Drew is so popular. But at the time I just couldn't believe that anyone would go to a birthday party for me! Nobody knows me. I feel so invisible when I'm at school!" Okay, I admit that at this point I was desperately attempting to make my parents feel sorry for me to ease the punishment, but it really wasn't that far from the truth.

"So you told Drew that it was okay to invite all her friends here while we were gone." My mom was not smiling, but her face was still her normal beige tone, so I took that as a good sign.

"No! She said that we should each just invite one person, she and Carmen and I, and we would see what happened from there. The person that Carmen invited didn't even come!"

"Who did you invite?" Dad chimed in. He was now flossing his teeth. It was so like Dad to get caught in a random and unnecessary detail.

"No one." And that was the truth. I didn't have anyone to invite.

Mom was sitting straight up in her bed, her arms folded over her chest, and her lips taught. "And let me guess, Drew told the most popular kid in school, and he and his buddies all showed up?"

She was getting good at this. I nodded.

"Why were they only here for a half hour?" I could barely understand Dad, as he was talking again with two fingers and a string of floss in his mouth.

My head was bowed so low that I was speaking straight into my chest, "Jess came over and kicked everyone out."

Dad scratched the top of his head and tossed his floss in the trash can.

Mom was still except for one eyebrow that lifted high enough to reach her hairline. "I'm disappointed in you, Gemma."

That was the sentence I had been dreading all day, and my mom said it best. She was disappointed in me. It wasn't a big surprise, but it sounded terrible said out loud.

I wanted her to yell at me. I wanted her to tell me I was grounded for a year. But she just stared at the air between us, looking older than I had ever seen her look before.

"Thank you for telling us the truth. Your father and I will talk about what we think will be the best consequence for your actions, and we'll talk to you about it tomorrow." She didn't ease off from her seriousness for a moment. She was perfect at being firm. She scared the heck out of me.

I mumbled a good night and closed their door behind me. My heart was beating incredibly fast as I walked down the hall toward my room.

"Hey, loser," I heard Bridget's voice as I passed her room. I knew she was talking to me. I stopped and peeked around her half-opened door as she grumbled, "Get in here." I pushed the door open and walked up to the edge of her bed stand. She was sitting in her bed just like my mom, reading a big textbook. Her room was covered with Yale paraphernalia. Hanging from her walls were posters, banners, an old vintage sweater, the works. She had wanted to go to Yale to study law since she was born. She was definitely the intelligent one out of us two sisters.

"What?" I muttered the way a defensive little sister does to her big sister who just called her a loser.

"Since you're going to be doing my chores for the next year, I thought you might as well get started now by taking my dirty clothes down to the laundry room. Make sure you separate the darks from the whites."

I looked at her in amazement. "You heard me in there?"

"This house isn't that big, Gemma." She was looking at her textbook again. She and Mom were so much alike, except that Mom was caring and loving and kind.

"They won't get mad at you," I whined. "I'm the one they can't trust."

She snorted. "Oh trust me, I'm in trouble. Big trouble. You think they're going to see past the fact that there were thirty kids in the house while I was upstairs in my room minding my own business?" She snorted again. "No way. I'm probably in it deeper than you are. Not that I care. I'll be out of this house and living in the dorms in five months, but we made a deal and you're doing my chores—for a year."

I scowled. "You just said that you won't even be here for a year."

"Yeah, but all my things that I leave behind will need dusting. And I'll come home now and again with dirty laundry—that should give you plenty to do." She dipped her nose back into her book. I huffed and left her room. When I got to my room, it was dark. I didn't want to turn on the lights. I stood in the blackness for a minute, contemplating the whole weekend and how things had changed so dramatically in twenty-four hours. My parents couldn't trust me. My sister was my new master. Jess, my best friend, hated me and probably wouldn't ever talk to me again. And Drew, my only friend at school, who also probably wouldn't talk to me again after last night, was turning out to be not such a good friend after all. Life had been so much simpler a few months ago. I silently wished to be able to go back to that time.

I was still standing motionless between my closed door and my bed when I heard a small tap at my window. I darted out of my room so quickly that I forgot to switch on the light for a signal. I had been dying inside for the past twenty-four hours that we hadn't spoken to each other. I closed the back door carefully and tiptoed on the cold grass until I saw Jess staring up at my window with a handful of small rocks in his hand.

"Hey," I spoke cautiously. I was suddenly not sure if he had come to make peace with me or to reprimand me some more.

Jess was startled, but he looked happy to see me. He dropped the rocks in the flowerbed and walked toward me. "I didn't think you were going to come down."

I looked up at my window then back to him again. "I'm sorry for last night," I said. "I was mad about the dumb party and..."

Jess stepped toward me and placed the top of his index finger on my lips. "I didn't come here for an apology," he whispered. He was standing so close to me that I could feel his cool, minty breath on my cheeks.

"Why did you come then?" I asked when he lowered his finger from my mouth.

He didn't blink once as he stared at me with his crystal blue eyes, searching for what he wanted to say. When he finally spoke, his words were distinct and exaggerated, "I *hate* seeing you with other guys. When I walked in on you and Greg, about to kiss..." He shook his head at the memory. "... I went ballistic. I overreacted. I'm sorry."

I was surprised by Jess's confession of jealousy. It was a confession I had wanted him to make for such a long time, and now that he had, I wasn't quite sure what it meant. Did it mean that *he* wanted to kiss me? Or was it simply an explanation for his actions and nothing else? He was still standing so close to me, and he didn't take his eyes off mine for one moment. He raised his hand up once more and ever so gently rubbed the back of his fingers along the jaw line of my face. When his fingers reached my chin, he slowly dropped his hand and stepped away from me with a sigh. "Just for the record, why were you and Greg going to kiss in front of a room full of people?"

I nearly got whip lash from Jess's new direction of conversation. I could have sworn five seconds ago that he was going to kiss me, and now he was asking about Greg? It took me a second to gather my thoughts. "I don't know. I don't think he was really going to kiss me."

Jess looked confused. "It sure looked like he was going to kiss you from the angle that I was at."

I skimmed my fingers through my hair, and a million tiny strands fell back around my face. "No, it was just a game. He bet me a quarter that he could kiss me without touching me."

Jess looked up at the sky and rolled his eyes.

"What?" I asked innocently.

"The quarter kiss." Jess rubbed both of his hands over his face.

"The quarter kiss?" I repeated. "There's a name for it?"

"The guy bets the girl a quarter that he can kiss her without touching her—which is obviously impossible—then he kisses her, and when the kiss is over, he hands her the quarter since he lost the bet. So the girl gets a quarter, and the guy gets a kiss. It's stupid."

I looked away from Jess toward the pale yellow siding on our house as the information registered in my brain. "It was a *trick*,"

I said as the events from the night before unfolded in my mind. I started breathing heavier as anger filled my lungs and then my cheeks. "He was going to take advantage of me in front of all of those people!" I began to huff, and I could feel my face getting hot.

"Don't be too mad, Gemma. Greg's not such a bad guy; he just likes attention."

"How do you know him, anyway?"

Jess hesitated. "We kind of hang out with the same crowd."

My mouth dropped open. "So Drew was right?"

"It's not like we're good friends; we just happen to be friends with the same people."

"Is he a sophomore like you?"

"No, he's a senior."

"A senior?" I was almost flattered to think that a senior in high school almost kissed me. But then I remembered the trick, and a wave of nausea passed over me. "He's two years older than you. I don't know anyone two years older than me."

"That will change when you get into high school."

"So all those people that were here last night—you know all of them too?"

Jess took a deep breath. "It's not like they're assassins. They didn't know they were going to a *fake* birthday party."

"But the alcohol in the punch! You knew it was there without even tasting it!" It was all coming together in my head now. "Do you go to a lot of parties with *alcohol?*"

"You know me, Gemma. You know that I'm home with my mom and sisters on most weekend nights. And when I'm not with them, I'm with *you.* I don't go out and party with those people. But I'm friends with a lot of them at school. A lot of them are on my baseball team, and some of them are in my classes.

They don't all drink, but some of them do. I can't tell them how to live their lives. I just stay away from that side of them. But I know that some of them do it, especially Greg. So when I saw the punch in his hand—I just knew. He's a nice guy; he's just got some messed up priorities."

My arms were folded tightly over my chest by now, and I grunted as soon as Jess ended his speech. "Nice? I don't think a nice guy would trick a girl into kissing him."

"You could have said no, Gem. You are partly to blame, as much as you'd like to be the victim in this situation."

I thought about that for a minute. As much as it bugged me that he would claim that I wanted to be a victim, I kind of knew it was true.

He continued, "And I was probably a bit rough with those things I said about Drew. She's living in the shadow of her brother, and it makes sense that she feels like she needs to do things that are as elaborate and as noticeable as he is. And besides, you could have said no to her too."

I relaxed my shoulders and looked up at the night sky. "I could have said no to a lot of things."

"But you didn't, so I said no for you."

And that was how it had always been with me and Jess. He was the smart one, always ready to give me advice when I did something stupid. And I was the naïve one, always ready to be saved. And I had to wonder if that's all we would ever be. Why hadn't he kissed me? Why was I always making such idiotic decisions? Why would Jess want to be with someone like me? Then it occurred to me that maybe Jess's closeness, his soft touches, and his long stares had absolutely nothing to do with him wanting a relationship. Maybe that was just his way of taking care of me.

chapter seventeen

I fully expected to be mocked and scorned when I returned to school on Monday. But when everything seemed normal, I remembered that besides Drew and Carmen, everyone at my house on Friday night was in high school. That made me feel older than I was. I wasn't sure how things were between Drew and me. I wasn't sure if she was mad at me for the way the party turned out. I wasn't even sure if I was mad at her for the way it all turned out. I wanted to be mad at her, but just like Jess had said, she wasn't entirely to blame.

"Hey!" I tried to sound as casual as possible as I approached Drew and Carmen at our locker before first period. Drew was emptying the contents of her backpack into the locker while Carmen carefully applied lip gloss in a portable mirror she held in her hand. Both of them seemed surprised to see me.

"Hey," they both said simultaneously, though the emotion behind their greeting was lacking.

I reached over Drew's head to grab my geometry book and asked how their weekends were. Neither of them answered me, but they watched me with careful eyes. I leaned up against the wall next to our locker and pretended not to notice. "It got warm this weekend. I can't wait for summer." Nice, I brought up the weather. Could I be any more awkward? But I had to say something.

Drew looked at Carmen then back at me. "We don't think it's a good idea that you share our locker anymore."

"Are you serious?" I stared at Drew with my entire face scrunched up around my eyes. She must have been joking. I thought she might be a little bothered about Friday night, but to entirely end our friendship? The whole stupid fake birthday party was *her* idea!

"Things were just so weird the other night." Drew replied without looking at me.

Then Carmen added, "It left a bad taste in our mouths." That was one of the first times Carmen had actually spoken to me directly.

"You have got to be kidding me." I glared at Drew. "*You're* the one that came up with the fake birthday party. *You're* the one that invited half the high school. And *you're* the one that asked your brother to kiss me!" I was yelling now and slowly becoming aware of the passing students that were turning their heads toward the commotion.

"You could have said no, Gem" Drew muttered into the stack of books she was holding against her chest.

"Why does everyone keep telling me that? There were a *ton* of people around! Most of which were very good-looking high school boys! So I gave into peer pressure! I'm fifteen! It's my *job* to give into peer pressure!"

Drew looked around the hall like she was bored with the conversation. "Sorry, Gem. It was just too … weird."

I glared hard at the side of her head. She may not have been able to see it, but I knew she could feel it. "Why did you even become friends with me? Was it so you could humiliate me? Did you just see me as an easy target to belittle and boost your self-esteem?" And at that moment I knew. I knew why she had started talking to me. I knew why she had made me her new best friend. I couldn't believe I hadn't thought of it before. "You used me to get to Trace Weston, didn't you?" Drew shifted her feet uncomfortably, and Carmen stood next to her like a bodyguard. "That's it, isn't it? You thought I was friends with him, and you thought you could get to him through me. Well, I've got news for you. Not only did you not get Trace, you just lost *me!*"

Drew and Carmen stepped out of my way while I hastily pulled from the locker what belonged to me—two textbooks and an old granola bar. I slammed the locker shut and marched down the hall while Drew and Carmen watched with looks of shock plastered to their faces. When I was twenty feet down the hall, I turned around one last time.

"And *don't* call me *Gem!*"

I walked—no, ran—toward my first-period classroom, but I couldn't go in. Instead I flew past the door and headed straight for the girl's bathroom. Tears were streaming down my face by this point, so I ducked my head as I weaved in and out of the hundreds of girls crammed in front of the bathroom mirrors. I slipped into the only available stall—the handicap stall at the very back of the room. I sat down on the toilet seat—even though my pants were still on—and wept into my backpack. How could this happen to me? This was a hundred times worse than I had imagined it. I thought Drew and I were friends! But she was turning out to be the most terrible, self-centered, inconsiderate person I knew! The first-period bell rang and the bathroom grew quiet. Soon I was alone, which only made it easier to cry. I cried because of the rejection. I cried because of the shock of the rejection. But most of all, I cried because of my stupidity. Why had I ever wanted to be friends with Drew? She used me from the very beginning. How could I allow her to have a huge party at my house when my parents were out of town? Was I *that* weak? And to think that I almost turned on Jess because of her! Was having no friends at school really so bad that I had to go and make friends with the twenty-first century version of Cruella Devil?

I heard another bell ring, which meant first period was over. I wiped at my eyes and pulled myself together enough to be able to finally exit the stall. I made it to second period and then to third and onto the rest until the final bell rang. And then finally, I made it home. I stepped through our front door and clumsily dropped my backpack on the steps. The house was filled with its usual smells of my mom cooking in the kitchen, and I followed the smells until I got to the kitchen counter, where I fell heavily into the bar stool and waited for Mom to ask me what was wrong. She was stirring something in a pot on the stove, and it took her longer to speak than I had expected.

"I'm worried about you." The words themselves made sense since I was basically having the worst week of my life, but the tone of her voice created a knot the size of Rhode Island in my stomach. She was mad.

I lifted my head off the counter and watched the back of her as she stood motionless, staring into the pot in front of her. "What do you mean?" I needed an explanation. I was going crazy not knowing what would make her so angry that instead of yelling at me she was giving me something close to the silent treatment. We hadn't talked much since my confession to her the night before. She seemed pretty normal at breakfast, though she did mention that we were going to discuss the "consequences of my actions" tonight after dinner. But even then she didn't seem angry. Not like this.

She turned around slowly as she rested the spoon on a plate next to the stove. She stared at me with cold, hard eyes as she lifted up her hands. She pointed to the index finger on her left hand with the index finger from her right. "First, you throw a party in our home when your father and I aren't in town and when we had specifically said you could only have two friends over." She paused and pointed to her middle finger. "Second, you snuck out of the house to go talk to Jess *after* you were already in trouble." She pointed to her ring finger next. "Then to top it all off I get a call from your principal—for the second time this year—telling me that you skipped first period today!" Her eyes were huge, and I could have sworn I saw a blood vessel pop in her forehead. "Is there something going on with you that I don't know about?"

I opened my mouth, but no words came out.

So Mom went on, "Do you honestly think that I have nothing else in my life to worry about? Do you think that things are just so darn easy that you need to skip school and throw parties so I have something to *do?*"

I could feel the tears pressing their way up toward my eyes again, and I knew I couldn't hold them in. I began to sob for the zillionth time that day. "I didn't mean to skip first period!"

"Oh! You didn't *mean* to skip first period." Mom bounced on her hip as she continued on with her sarcastic dramatization. "Well, as long as you didn't *mean* to skip first period, then I guess it's *okay!*" She suddenly remembered whatever was in the pot that was starting to boil. She picked up the spoon and started stirring furiously.

"It's true, Mom, I didn't mean to skip class." The tears were strolling down my cheeks faster now. "It was just such a terrible day!" I buried my head in my arms.

"Oh, let me guess. Did you forget your class schedule and go sit by the dumpster all day? Oh wait, that already *happened!*"

I didn't know Mom had it in her to be so sarcastic. She hated it when Bridget and I were sarcastic. She always said it was the devil's humor.

I lifted my head and looked at her in awe. I couldn't believe I had actually brought my mom to her snapping point. I had gone too far.

"Mom, I—"

"No! I don't want to hear it right now. Just go up to your room!"

I waited for her to change back to the mom I knew. I waited for her to put her arms around me and tell me everything was going to work out all right. But she didn't, so I finally slunk off of the bar stool like an earthworm and dragged myself up the stairs to my room. I closed the door behind me and walked directly into the closet. I closed the closet door behind me and crawled in the darkness through my church dresses until I reached mine and

Jess's wall. I curled my legs up to my chest as tight as they would go, and then I cried myself to sleep.

I woke up sometime later to the sound of loud voices.

"What do you mean she's not in here?" It was Mom, and she was still yelling.

Then I heard Dad's calm, even voice. "Are you sure she came up here?"

"Yes! I told her to come up here an hour ago!" Her voice became low and bitter. "So help me if she snuck out again! I have had it up to *here* with that girl!" I could imagine Mom holding her hand up to her forehead as she said it. I was about to reveal myself to my parents until I realized that Mom was now crying. Dad made hushed, soothing tones, and I was sure he had his arms around her. Her words were broken and came intermittently between the sobs. And though they were muffled by the flannel shirt that covered Dad's chest, I heard her words clearly when she said, "Oh, Rob, how… am I going to raise her… without you?"

chapter eighteen

I shut my eyes again and cuddled closer to the closet wall. I suppose I was trying to get as far away from everything as I could. My thoughts rolled through my brain like a bingo machine as I considered the possible meaning to my mom's words. Why would she have to raise me without my dad? Divorce was the first possibility that came to my mind. Before Jess's parents got divorced, it was something that seemed to only happen in far off places like Los Angeles or New York. Not in my world. But since the reality of Caris and Kevin Tyler set in, I had realized that there were a lot more divorced parents than I ever knew about. Drew's parents were divorced. I knew because Drew mentioned once that she was going to visit her dad in Atlanta for the summer. And I thought Carmen's parents were divorced because whenever she talked about her home, she called it "my mom's house." The idea of my parents not being married anymore created a lump the size of a billiard ball in my throat. I wanted to cry again, but I didn't have any more tears to cry.

I realized then that there were other possibilities beyond divorce. Maybe he was going on a long trip. Maybe he had gotten a job offer in Germany or France or some far away country and we would only be able to see him on holidays and a summer vacation. That would be sad, but it would be a much better option than divorce. The second option made me feel lighter, and I finally found the strength to lift myself up off the carpet and crawl out of the dark closet into my bedroom. The sun had set and only a tiny bit of blue light shown through my windows. How long had I been in there? I opened my bedroom door and stepped into the lit hallway. I blinked at the sharpness of the light and rubbed my swollen eyes. I could hear my parents and Bridget in the kitchen, utensils hitting plates, and ice bumping against the water glasses. They had gone ahead and eaten dinner without me.

I walked into the kitchen feeling like an outsider in my own family. I stopped at the doorway and watched as Bridget dished herself up a second helping of lasagna, my favorite meal. Dad was the only one to look up at me.

"Hey, Gem, where have you been?" His mouth was turned upward, but his face didn't look happy. I could tell that he was trying to keep himself on an even playing field between me and Mom, but he wasn't going to be able to stay there for long. He always succumbed to Mom's side of the battle. Not because he always agreed, but because he was a loyal husband.

"I fell asleep in my closet," I mumbled. They were the first words I had spoken since I was sentenced to my room by Mom. The words came out with a grumble in my throat.

Bridget snorted as she took a bite of green beans. Mom put her fork down and wiped her mouth with a napkin.

"You should eat, Gemma," Mom spoke softly without looking at me, "while it's still hot."

Part of me wasn't hungry, but part of me was starving. I think the part of me that was starving was also the part of me that ached for normalcy with my family. I loved lasagna, and I longed to be able to enjoy it while laughing with my parents about my day at school or listening to Bridget tell about a date she had to go on that weekend even though she really didn't want to.

I slid into my usual chair at the table as Bridget continued telling my parents a story about her biology class that I had apparently interrupted.

"So Sandra goes up to Mr. Kroff and asks why she got a B minus on her report card when she's gotten As on all of her tests." I stared at Bridget, even though I was barely listening to her, and it occurred to me that her world really hadn't changed that much. To her this was just a family dinner like any other night. She wasn't in big trouble like I was. And she didn't overhear Mom say something to Dad that wasn't supposed to be heard. "Then Mr. Kroff tells her—in front of the whole class—that she was tardy nine times this semester, and he takes two percent off your grade every time you are tardy! Can you believe that? Two percent! That really adds up!" Bridget looked around the table with wide eyes, even though the rest of us were staring at our forks, emotionless. "Sandra was the only one in the class getting a better grade than me. So you know what that means." Bridget took another bite of green beans then continued, "I'm the top of my class."

At that Dad seemed to beam back into the present day from wherever his thoughts had taken him. "Wow, Bridge! That's great! Congratulations!"

I knew he hadn't heard a word of the story before that, but Bridget was beaming with delight. Bridget took another big bite of her food, and there was a long stretch of complete silence while she chewed. Mom barely looked up from her plate, and Dad only looked up to reach for the salt and pepper. I ate quietly, though the lasagna didn't taste nearly as good as it usually did. The tension between my parents and I was thick, and the silence was making everything taste worse with each bite. I couldn't take it any longer.

I looked at Mom, who was watching her green beans as she pushed them around her plate. "Why are you going to have to raise me without Dad?" I didn't mean to yell.

Mom's head shot up and stared at me in shock across the table. Dad looked at me with as much astonishment until he turned to my mom and put his hand on her arm.

Bridget broke the silence, "What are you talking about, Gemma?" Panic filled her eyes as she saw everyone's expressions. She looked back at Dad. "*What* is she talking about?"

Dad took in a deep breath and looked at Mom questioningly, but she didn't take her eyes off of me. "Maybe you two girls should go upstairs and do your homework. Your mom and I will clean up down here."

"What's going on?" Bridget pushed. I remained silent. I had already done enough.

Dad spoke again when it became obvious that Mom wasn't going to. "Let your mom and I have a moment down here, Bridget. I'll come up and talk to you both in a minute."

Bridget threw her napkin on her plate and pushed her chair out from behind her. It squeaked as it slid across the linoleum. She marched up the stairs as loudly as she could, and I followed sheepishly behind her. I walked into my bedroom; the sun was far beneath the surface of the earth, and the only thing coming through the windows now was the dim glow of street lights below. I didn't have the courage to turn on the lights. I folded down the comforter on my bed as well as the sheet below. With my shoes still on, I slid safely underneath them, pulling them far over my head. I didn't see the light come on some moments later, but I felt a warm hand brush over my back that was followed by the cool tone of Dad's voice.

"Gemma, sweetheart." He sounded sad. "Would you come on downstairs? Your mother and I need to talk to you and your sister about something."

I unfolded the sheets, revealing my face that was covered with matted hair. "Before we go down there," I urged, "please just promise me one thing."

Dad's eyes looked bigger than I had ever seen them. He didn't say anything; he didn't even nod, but I continued.

"Don't leave us." The familiar sting of salt built up behind my eyes. "I'm sorry for everything I've done. Just tell me that you won't leave us."

Dad said nothing. Instead he reached out for my hand and led me out of my room and down the stairs to the living room, where Mom and Bridget were already sitting, waiting. The silence in the room was almost tangible, like it was waiting for the right moment to pounce on me and make breathing an impossibility. When we were all sitting down—Mom and Dad on one couch, Bridget and I facing them on the other—Dad started to speak.

"Girls, there is something that Mom and I need to tell you."

"Wait!" I pleaded. I couldn't let Dad tell us whatever terrible news he had to tell us while there was such tension between Mom and me. The air had to be clear or else the new news would swallow me whole. "I'm sorry for everything the past couple days. I'm sorry about the party, and I'm sorry for sneaking out. I'm sorry that I skipped class, and I'm sorry that I fell asleep in the closet." I barely took a breath. I kept rambling my apologies off so that no one could interrupt me before I was finished. "I didn't skip class on purpose today. Drew told me she didn't want to be friends with me after what happened Friday night, and I was crying so hard that I had to go to the bathroom to clean up. I know it's a lame excuse, but I'm not purposely skipping class. I'm not being rebellious on purpose or anything like that. I'm just making some really dumb mistakes." I was looking at Mom, who was watching me with kind, wet eyes. "I'm still me. I'm still Gemma. I'm sorry."

Mom leaned forward and reached for my knee. "I know, honey. I knew that all along. I just haven't been myself lately. I'm sorry too."

And with that, the air was cleared. I was able to take in a solid, deep breath for the first time since my parents got back from their trip. The tension between Mom and me, between Dad and me, even between Bridget and me, was obliterated in that instant, leaving room for a brand new dilemma that was rising to the surface.

"Girls," Dad picked up right where he had left off, "I'm sick." His words came like a semi truck directly at my forehead, and I felt whiplash from the blow. We've all been sick with the flu or a cold; Bridget even had pneumonia when she was twelve, but this was different. The way my parents watched us while Dad was talking made me realized that this wasn't a sickness that would be cured by Tylenol or Amoxicillin. I doubted that Dad was even referring to a sickness that would require surgery before he would be well. Somewhere deep inside I knew this was different. It was much worse.

Bridget was the first one to react. "What do you mean you're sick? Sick with what?" She sounded defensive, but I didn't know why.

Mom was the one to answer. "Your father has something called small cell lung cancer. It is an aggressive disease, but the doctors are doing everything they can to help him."

Cancer. The word meant the same to me as tsunami or piranha. I had never seen them; I wasn't even quite sure what they were, but I knew they were bad. And I knew in many cases, they were deadly.

I could barely move let alone reply to what I had just heard. Bridget, on the other hand, was angry. "You have *cancer?* How long have you known about this?" She was off the couch and red faced, yelling loudly at both of my parents, mostly at Dad.

"Have a seat, Bridget. We're going to talk about this calmly." Dad's voice was even, as though he had expected this reaction from her. Bridget hesitantly sat back on the couch, clutching tightly to a pillow. Dad continued, "I went in for a chest exam about two months ago. I was having a hard time breathing, and I thought it might be asthma."

Mom picked up the explanation from there; it wasn't strange for them to bounce off each other like that. "The doctor found a lump in your father's chest. He ran some tests and found a malignant tumor."

I didn't know what that meant either, but the force at which Bridget etched her fingernails into the pillow she was holding told me it was bad.

Dad continued from there, "Doctor Howe, our oncologist, suggested we go to a special hospital in Jacksonville that does a lot of work with cancer patients. He thought maybe they would have some better ideas of how to get me better. They had good news for us."

Bridget sat up straighter. "You told us you went to Jacksonville for work!"

"I know we did, Bridge." Dad looked down at his hands. "We wanted to find out as much as we could about this before we told you and Gemma. We wanted to be able to give you as much information as possible."

"So stop lying to us then and give us the information!"

I turned to Bridgett and yelled, "He would if you would stop interrupting him!" She jerked away from me and melted into her pillow. I was surprised that she let it go so easily.

"The tumor hasn't started spreading yet, and the doctors at the Mayo clinic think that radiation and chemotherapy could do a lot of good in my situation."

Bridget was back on guard and ready to fight. "So how long do you have to live?"

"Bridget!" Mom gasped. I felt nauseated and wanted to crawl onto Mom's lap and burrow myself in the safety of her arms.

"What?" Bridget's eyes looked like daggers as she turned to Mom. "We deserve to know how long he's going to be around! I deserve to know if he's going to be alive when I get married or when I graduate from *high school!*"

Mom began to sob. Big, wet, alligator tears streamed down her cheeks and around her jaw line. She didn't wipe at them; she just let them fall as she stared blankly into the face of her oldest daughter.

"Bridget, I know this is hard on you," Dad began, but again he was cut short by Bridget's raging temper.

"No, you don't! You don't know how hard this is! You didn't just find out that your father is dying and he's known for two months and never told you! You didn't just find out that you're going to be the one raising your little sister because your mom is going to be in a state of depression when you're gone! You weren't just sentenced to a life of living at home so you can glue back the pieces of your messed-up family! You don't know what it's like! You *don't* know what it's *like!*" Bridget stepped over me in a fit of tears and ran up the stairs before any of us knew what happened. Mom was still staring at the empty space on the couch where Bridget had been sitting. Dad was whispering calming words in her ear and rubbing her back. He then looked up at me.

"Gemma, how are you doing with all of this? I know we bombarded you with a lot of information. Do you have any questions?"

Did I have any questions? Only a million. Was he going to die? And if so, when? And when he did die, what would life be like? And where would he go? Would he be gone forever, or just floating in the clouds somewhere waiting for the rest of us? But I shook my head. "No."

chapter nineteen

I used to play in Jess's backyard every day. It was home to many of our tree forts and the make-believe coliseum for our endless wrestling matches and soccer games. But it had been a while since we had played back there. The last time recently that I had been in his backyard was last summer for the Fourth of July when Caris invited our family over for a barbeque. But even when it got dark on that night, his yard was filled with voices and laughter and spitting sparklers. Tonight it was dark and quiet and only vaguely familiar. I didn't sneak out to get there. It wasn't even eight o'clock when my parents both quietly ascended the staircase—I assumed to talk to Bridget—so I told them I had to go out for a minute. They only nodded and continued up the stairs. They knew as well as I did where I was going.

I searched in the dark for some small rocks to lob at Jess's window. I looked up at the back of the big old house that Jess's mom had inherited from her grandmother. There were a dozen windows at least, but I had them memorized. I knew exactly which one was Jess's bedroom. I realized for the first time just how hard it was to find a rock the right size. They were either too small and wouldn't fly to the second story level of the house, or they were too big and I was risking breaking the window. I finally managed to find one, and it made a little smacking sound as it hit the window. It sounded so different from this angle outside than it did all the times I had heard the rock against the glass in my bedroom.

The pane of the window rattled, and I could see a dark figure through the glass. Soon the window was open, and Jess's twelve-year-old sister, Vivian, peered down at me from above—a look of consternation etched across her face.

"What are you doing here?" she asked, annoyed. I got along okay with Jess's sisters, but I had known for a while that they didn't like that Jess spent so much time with me. I guess they saw me as competition. To be honest, I didn't blame them. If I had a brother like Jess, I wouldn't want to share him either.

I ignored her question. "Is Jess home?"

Vivian scowled then ducked her head back inside and yelled Jess's name. Soon Jess's head was peering out of the window where Vivian's had once been. He squinted his eyes at me. "What are you doing down there?"

"This is how you always get me to come down and talk!" I yelled up to him, my neck stretched as far is it could go.

Jess bent his head back inside the window and looked at the watch on his wrist. "Gemma, it's barely eight o'clock. You could have just come to the front door."

"Could you just come down here?" I urged. My voice cracked, and Jess's expression changed from humored to concerned. In an instant the window was empty.

I wandered around the yard toward the back door. Caris had mentioned to my mom once that her husband, Kevin, had promised to someday put in a patio with a Jacuzzi. But between me and the back door was a bare slab of cement. That was one promise out of many that was never fulfilled.

Jess stepped through the sliding glass door and immediately walked toward me until he was close enough to wrap an arm around my shoulders. "What's the matter? Is everything okay?"

He had asked me this many times before when my problems had all been so trivial. I wished I was coming to him with a concern about a boy not liking me or an issue with a friend. But this was so much worse. So unfixable.

"Can we go for a walk?"

We walked in silence until we reached the cement jungle at the top of our street. It was harder to climb the blocks in the dark, but we had done it enough times that it came naturally. We sat dangling our feet from the highest stack of blocks. From this stack we could see over the rooftops and the tall pine trees and catch a glimpse of Emery Lake as it shimmered under the moonlight. It had been almost a year since Jess and I had sat there together. Though never before had he sat this close, with his arm wrapped around me so tightly.

Jess's voice broke the silence. "Is this about Drew?"

Drew? It took me a second to realize who he was talking about. It occurred to me that the girl belonging to that name had shattered my world only ten hours earlier. But now that seemed so insignificant.

"No, it's about my dad," I choked as I spoke.

"Your dad?" Jess squeezed me. The sides of our bodies were

perfectly aligned, and his warmth sent a chill down my spine. "What's wrong with him?"

"I think he's going to die." I said it matter-of-factly because I didn't know how else to say it.

"Is he hurt? What's wrong with him?"

I was trying to avoid the word. It seemed so encompassing. But it crept out of my mouth like a dying caterpillar. "Cancer."

Jess looked away from me and out toward the endless amount of trees. I could hear him breathing in and out until he finally responded, "What kind?"

I shook my head. "I don't know, some kind of lung cancer, I guess."

"Lung cancer," he said quietly as though he was talking to himself. "My grandpa had lung cancer."

"He *had* lung cancer?" I asked hopefully. "Did it go away?"

Jess looked at me with pained eyes. "No, he, uh … "

"Oh." I looked down at my hands. He didn't have to finish the sentence. His grandpa had died.

Jess pulled me even closer to him. "But he was old. Your dad's a lot younger," he whispered the words into my hair. "Your dad will fight this."

I didn't doubt what Jess was saying. My dad was tough, and he had a strong will to live. He *would* fight this. But would he win?

Jess unwrapped his arm from around my shoulders and rested back on his hands. I felt cold without him right up against me. "How did you find out?" he asked.

"I fell asleep in my closet this afternoon, and my parents didn't know I was in there."

"You overheard them talking about it?"

"My mom asked my dad how she was going to raise me without him. So I asked them about it, and they told us he had cancer."

Jess grimaced. "I'm sorry." Then a look of confusion crossed his face. "Why were they talking about that in *your* room?"

"They came to get me for dinner."

"But you were asleep in the closet."

"Uh huh."

"Why were you asleep in the closet again?"

"My mom got really mad at me for skipping class and sneaking out with you last night, so she sent me to my room, and I just wanted to be alone in a dark place, so I went into the closet."

"You skipped class again?"

"Not on purpose. I was crying and didn't want to go to first period with tears running down my face."

"Why were you crying?"

I was amazed at how far behind Jess was in the goings-on of my life.

"Because Drew kicked me out of her locker and told me she didn't want to be my friend anymore because of how the fake birthday party turned out."

"Seriously?" Jess seemed bothered.

I nodded as I stared blankly ahead.

"Wow. That girl just gets better every day," he grumbled.

"It doesn't really matter anymore." I sat motionless, staring at the blackness ahead of me. Nothing seemed to matter anymore. Friends, boys, school… they all seemed so petty, so pointless. "What will I do if he dies?"

Jess replied quietly, "I don't know."

"What did you do?"

"What do you mean? My dad didn't die."

"No, but he's not really in your family anymore."

"Yeah, but that's a good thing. There were so many years of him corrupting the whole feeling of our home that once he was gone we were happy."

"I wonder if it will be that way for us. I wonder if he'll just get sicker and sicker, and it will finally get to the point that we *want* him to die."

Jess didn't have a response. For the first time in our friendship Jess didn't have any advice for my predicament. He had never had a parent diagnosed with cancer. He didn't know what it felt like, and he wasn't about to pretend to. I offered a new subject. "What's going on with your dad and the custody issue?"

"My dad's lawyer thinks he should get us for the summer and every other holiday. But we're hoping that I can just go, so the girls won't have to leave my mom."

I jerked my head around. "Does your dad's lawyer know that he's an abusive jerk?"

Jess shook his head. "I guess because it was the first time he ever showed physically abusive behavior, they're letting him off pretty easy. He had sixty days in jail, and he's pretty much off the hook."

"So what now," I was starting to get angry, and my words were defensive, "you're just going to be gone all summer with your dad?"

"Maybe, I don't know." Jess didn't look up from his hands.

I was frustrated at Jess's apathetic response. "Where does he even live?"

"He moved back to where he grew up. I think he's sharing an apartment right now with my uncle."

"Where did he grow up? Is it far away?" I couldn't imagine a summer without Jess. We always spent every second together at the lake, the snow cone shack... it didn't matter, we were always together. I couldn't bear to face the school break without him.

Jess looked up toward the lake and rubbed his hand over his hair. His expression was still and lacking in emotion as he answered, "California."

As the days and weeks passed, my dad didn't look much different. I suppose I expected him to start losing his hair like the people with cancer in the movies. I thought he'd start looking feeble and old and inherit a hunched back or something. But he looked completely normal. He was tired. Oftentimes when I returned home from school in the afternoon he was already home lying on the couch with a blanket draped over him. But for the most part he was just the same old Dad. I thought the fact that nothing had changed would bring me comfort, but instead it was the exact opposite. It only confused me more, and confusion is never comfortable.

Neither is rejection. I hadn't spoken to Drew for over a month. I sat on the opposite side of the room from her in German and did everything I could do to avoid her locker as I walked from class to class, which meant I was spending a lot more time at my own assigned locker in the dreaded eighth grade hall.

I needed to stop there before heading home, and as I passed all the unfamiliar eighth-grade faces, a tornado of fluttering butterflies swirled around my stomach when I saw Trace Weston standing at his locker. Even though I had been using my own locker for a while, I had only seen Trace a couple of times.

I approached my locker and started turning the combination lock. I could smell the sweet aroma of Trace's cologne—he was probably the only boy in junior high that could wear cologne and get away with it. I finished the combination and lifted the locker handle. *Darn!* It was still locked. I hated it when I got the combination wrong. Those lockers were so temperamental, and of course I would struggle with it the one time all week that Trace was at his locker!

I started again from the beginning, twisting the lock a few times to make sure it was reset. I turned the knob to thirty-seven, then turned it the other way one and a half times to nine, then back the final time to seventeen. I took a deep breath. *Please open. Please open. Please open.* I lifted the handle. Still locked! I shook the handle with a grunt of frustration. From the corner of my eye, I could see Trace put his last book in his backpack and zip it up. He was going to walk away, and I was going to be stranded here looking like the moron that couldn't open her own locker!

Trace closed his locker smoothly. It barely made a sound as it clicked into place. He lingered for a moment before clearing his throat. "Uh ... " He was facing me when the sound came out of his mouth. Was he actually talking to me? Was Trace Weston actually talking to *me?* "Gemma, I think you are trying to open the wrong locker."

"What?" I looked at him with the most utterly disgraceful look of confusion, and then I turned back to the locker handle that I was holding between my fingers. He was right. I was one locker off. In my nervous and excited state, I had actually gone to the *wrong* locker! And failed at opening it! *Twice!*

Humiliation swept over my body as I let my head fall against the locker that wasn't mine. "It's been a long day," I muttered mostly to myself—not thinking that Trace really even cared. I was amazed to find him still standing next to me when I finally lifted my head again.

"All the lockers look exactly the same." He was smiling and leaning casually against his locker as he spoke. "I went to the wrong locker about five times during my first couple weeks here."

I couldn't believe what was happening. Besides the one moment in the hall when he teased me about the German video, we had never said a word to each other—not ever. "Yeah, you'd think they'd paint them different colors or something," I answered hesitantly. I kept waiting for him to decide that I was boring or annoying and walk off down the hall.

"Or write our names on them at least." He chuckled at his joke, and I thought he looked cuter than he ever had before.

"I would need mine in big flashing letters," I added.

"Maybe a neon sign. Or an audible voice recorder calling your name." He cupped his hands around his mouth and pretended to talk through a speaker, "Gemma Mitchell, your locker is right *here.* No, you're at the wrong locker, Gemma. *This* is your locker; the bright purple one with the neon sign!"

I didn't know what surprised me more; the fact that he was so funny, or that he knew my full name. Wasn't this the same guy that rejected me at last year's Valentine's dance? The same guy who had said two words to me during an entire year of German together? Why was he now suddenly deciding to acknowledge my existence?

"I liked your movie in German class a while back."

"Oh, thanks." I blushed. "It was Drew that made it so great."

"I don't know. You have some pretty wicked dance moves." He snapped his fingers and pretended to dance in a retro style. "And that dress was awesome. It must have cost you a *fortune.*"

"It was my mom's!" I shouted. "I swear! I didn't buy that ugly thing!" I felt myself actually feeling at ease around him. I couldn't believe how natural it felt to laugh and joke around with Trace Weston. I opened the locker that *was* mine and got out what I needed while Trace asked me how long I had lived in Franklin.

"Forever." I pulled my backpack over my shoulders, and we started walking down the hall. "I was born here. How about you?" As if I didn't know.

"We moved here a year and a half ago from Michigan. My dad got transferred here for his job." We were walking down the main hall now toward the front doors of the school. I felt curious eyes on us as we passed. Trace continued, "We thought we were going to move back to Michigan this summer. We were all packed up and everything. But the day before school started, my dad got a call that we were staying here for another year."

"Hence, the eighth-grade hall locker." I gave him a humorous glance from the corner of my eye.

"Yeah, I guess." He cocked his head to the side. "What's your excuse?"

"Oh, I requested it," I joked. "I get along better with people who are shorter than me. It makes me feel better about myself."

Trace looked confused, so I quickly told him the truth. "No, my family is always in Cape Cod during registration So every year I get the locker that nobody else wants."

"What about your seventh grade year? Where did they put you then?"

"Back in the elementary," I joked. Trace's eyes sparkled at my humor. "It was so weird being back there sharing a cubby hole with a sixth grader."

Trace shook his head as he opened the front door of the school and waved for me to pass through in front of him.

As soon as we got outside, Trace squinted his eyes toward the line of buses. "My bus is here." He almost sounded disappointed. Then he looked back down at me. "It was nice talking with you, though. I hadn't seen you at the lockers for so long that I thought you had changed yours or something."

He had *noticed* that I wasn't there. "But you see me every day in German class. Why don't you ever talk to me?"

Trace lifted his hands in defense, "Why don't you ever talk to *me?*"

Um, hello? Do the words *last dance* ring a bell? But I was too embarrassed to say that out loud. So I said, "I think I thought you were too popular for me to talk to."

He grunted, "I'm not popular. I'm the dorky new kid that no one talks to."

"But everybody talks *about* you. Everybody thinks you're so cute and the dancer girls all call you 'Tray' like you're their prized poodle or something!"

Trace gripped his notebook. "The kid that everyone talks *about* but no one talks *to.*" Then he shrugged. "I'd rather be the kid that nobody talks about but a few people talk to."

He shifted uncomfortably from foot to foot, waiting for me to reply, but something else had caught my attention. It was Drew and Carmen. They were sitting on the grass by the carpool pick-up lane. They were watching us so intently that they seemingly had no plans of averting their gaze even after I made eye contact with them.

"What are you looking at?" Trace asked as he turned around to follow my eyes. Only then did Drew and Carmen turn their heads away from us. Trace looked back at me with a concerned expression. "What's going on with you and Drew? I thought you guys were good friends."

"*Were* being the operative word," I replied dryly.

"What happened?"

"I don't know. I…"

"Oh, no. My bus is leaving!" Trace cut me off mid-sentence. "I'm sorry. I really want to talk to you more." He looked toward his bus then back at me. "Do you want to hang out this weekend or something?"

The same tornado of butterflies that had invaded my stomach at the lockers was back. *Hang out?* With *Trace Weston?* I was excited and absolutely terrified at the same time. "Uh," I stuttered, "sure. Yeah. That would be fun."

Trace looked at my face as though he were trying to figure out what that meant. But he was in too big of a hurry to analyze it. "Okay," he replied. "I'll get your cell number tomorrow, and then I'll text you or something."

I nodded nervously. The world was spinning around my head.

"I better go."

I nodded stupidly again, and he ran off to catch his bus. What had just happened? I had never ever hung out with a guy before. Not a guy that wasn't Jess. And my first time was going to be with Trace Weston? I had to do something. I had to tell someone. I grabbed hold of my backpack straps and ran toward home.

chapter twenty

I actually wasn't all that surprised when Drew made her way to the seat next to me in German class the next day. It was the last twenty minutes of class, and we were supposed to be quietly working on our homework assignment. But Drew didn't think that rules applied to her.

"Hey," she said in a low tone.

I didn't look at her. I just stared deeply at my assignment.

"Hey," she repeated. I could tell from the corner of my eye that she was staring at me with those dark, piercing eyes.

I finally decided that I had to say something. But I was still angry and hurt, and I wanted to punish her. "What?" I mumbled, still looking at the paper in front of me.

"Are we seriously going to stay mad at each other forever?"

I looked at her in shock. "*You* are the one that didn't want to be friends with *me!*"

"I know." She dropped her head for a moment. "I really do feel bad about that."

"Are you kidding me, Drew?" I couldn't believe I was saying this, but I was so mad at her, I couldn't hold it in.

"What?" Her eyes were wide and confused.

"You are so obvious! You saw me talking to Trace yesterday, and now you want to be my friend again!"

"That's not it."

I had to give her credit; she was either a really good actor, or she was genuinely hurt by the accusation. "Then why? Why are you suddenly so keen on being friends with me?"

Drew pulled at the piece of gum in her mouth as she gathered her words. "I made a mistake. I'm sorry."

I waited for her to say more. That wasn't enough for me to just drop everything and become friends with her again.

She let go of her gum and leaned forward with her elbows on her knees. "Look, I felt so stupid after the party. I felt stupid that I got you in trouble. I felt stupid that my brother and his friends brought alcohol. I felt stupid that Jess found out, and I'm sure he hates me now. And I don't know, I just—"

"You thought you'd feel better if you ditched me."

She sat back with a sad expression. "It didn't work."

"Girls!" Frau Fart's voice pierced through our conversation. "If you don't have any homework to do right now, I can certainly assign you more."

Drew didn't even look at Frau Fart, but she ducked her head toward me and said, "Friends?"

I didn't have much time to think about it, so I went with what came naturally. "Sure, I guess." I took a quick look at Frau Fart before turning back to my homework.

Drew got up to go back to her desk but then turned back to me in the last second.

"What are you doing this weekend?" she whispered.

I thought about Trace. Did she already know what I was doing that weekend?

When I didn't respond, she continued, "Will you come to my house on Friday? I'm inviting a few people to play games and stuff."

"I'm not sure. I told Trace I'd hang out with him this weekend."

I studied her reaction carefully. Her eyebrows shot up, and she genuinely looked surprised. "You're hanging out with Trace? Are you two like ... going out?"

I was thrown off by her distressed expression. She was so vulnerable when it came to Trace. "No, we're just friends." I have no idea why I said the next part: "Do you want me to invite him to your house?"

Drew looked skeptical and hopeful at the same time. "You don't have to do that. That's not why ... "

I cut her off again, "It's okay, really. I can invite him." I was terrified of being alone with Trace that weekend. The idea of having other people around made the whole situation seem a thousand times less daunting.

She shrugged her shoulders. "If you want to. Does that mean you're coming?"

"Yeah, I'll come."

"Girls!" Frau Fart yelled louder this time.

Even Drew was startled by it as she jumped to her feet and whispered, "Be at my house by eight." Then she disappeared back to her desk.

On my way out of class, Trace came up behind me and tugged on my backpack strap. "Looked like you and Drew were having quite the conversation," he said with that familiar sparkle in his eye. I couldn't believe that we were talking again. I had somehow convinced myself that he would forget all about me, and I would go back to fantasizing about him from across the room for the rest of my life.

"Yeah," I replied, "it was really weird actually."

"What did she say?"

It felt strange telling Trace about my interaction with Drew before telling Jess. It felt weird telling anybody anything before telling Jess about it. "She kind of apologized, I guess, for everything that happened. She invited me over to her house Friday night to play games with some people. She said that you could come if you want."

Trace stuck out his bottom lip as he thought about the offer. Then with a nod of his head he said, "Sounds great. Do you want me to pick you up?"

His offer excited me and petrified me at the same time. To be picked up by Trace Weston felt like a dream, but the reality of it was a bit too much. Hanging out with him would be nerve racking enough without me having to deal with a doorstep scene. "No thanks, I'll just meet you at Drew's." A sick pit-like feeling developed in my stomach as I saw his eyes light up at the mention of Drew. He liked her. I just knew it. And now I was providing the perfect opportunity for them to be together this Friday night.

"I *hate* this!" I exclaimed as I dropped my books on the grass in front of my house after school.

Jess had been lying on the grass with his hands folded behind his head when I approached. "What happened?"

"Drew apologized to me today."

Jess sat up with surprise. "Really? That's huge. So what did you say?"

"I accepted it, I guess." My words lacked enthusiasm. "Then she invited me to her house this Friday to play games."

"Are you going to go?" He began playing with some grass, trying to make a whistle. But the grass was too wet, and it kept slipping between his fingers.

"Yes," I moaned under my breath. "I'm so stupid."

Jess looked up at me for an explanation.

"I told her I'd bring Trace."

"Why is that stupid?"

"Because she likes him, and I think he likes her too. And they're going to be all into each other, and I'm just going to be by myself looking like a loser."

"Why do you think Trace likes Drew?"

I shaded my eyes from the warm sun. "You've got to put the grass between your thumbs." I reached toward his hand that held the piece of grass and took it from him. "Like this." I held the grass taught between my lips and thumbs and blew. A high-pitched squeal escaped behind the grass.

Jess looked sincerely impressed. "Where did you learn to do that?"

"When we go up to the Cape, my mom always has a spa day where she goes and gets a massage and a mud bath and the whole works. So my dad takes Bridget and me to the same park that is close to the spa. It's an absolutely terrible park for kids. There's only one set of monkey bars and an old weedy sandbox." I paused to laugh at the irony.

"But according to my dad, the park has perfect conditions for making whistles. He calls it *whistle grass*."

Jess tried blowing into the grass once more. "How long would your mom be gone?"

"All afternoon. But we have fun. I always look forward to that day actually. Especially the past few years since Bridget has been old enough to go with my mom. I've gotten my dad all to myself." That's when I had a thought that made the whole Drew-slash-Trace situation insignificant.

"What's wrong?" Jess asked, still trying to straighten his thumbs around the grass blade.

"We're never going to go to Cape Cod again."

Jess sat perfectly still as he witnessed my realization.

"We're never going to have another family trip. My dad is too weak to go to the grocery store, let alone another state." I hated that this happened, but tears began forming in the corner of my eyes.

Jess leaned forward and stroked a piece of my hair that had fallen over my shoulder.

I continued, choking on my words, "Last year when we were making whistles, he told me that next year I would be old enough to go have spa day with the girls. When I told him that I preferred to be with him at the park, he was so happy." Tears began pouring out of my eyes. "He was so happy, Jess."

I heard Jess take a deep breath. I knew he didn't know what to say. I didn't either. It was just the way it was. My life had been perfect once, and now it was in ruins.

"So, Jess, who is your mother out with tonight?" Mom asked that night at dinner. Jess's sisters were at their grandma's again, and his mom had gone on her first date since the divorce. So Mom had insisted that Jess eat dinner at our house. To have him over again, for dinner with my family, was like Christmas all over again.

"It's actually kind of a funny story," Jess replied, but he wasn't smiling, "Parent-teacher conferences were last week at my school and—"

Bridget jumped in, "Your mom is going out with one of your teachers?" She threw her head back with an amused cackle, and I punched her in the arm.

Jess shifted in his chair. "No, nothing like that. But he's the dad of one of my friends at school. It was just weird to have him show up at my door all dressed up, holding flowers, you know." He stared at the ice in his glass.

Mom reached out and touched Jess's arm. "It would probably be a little strange to see any man other than your father showing up at your door for your mom, but I think this will be really good for her."

I watched Mom carefully scoop a bite of food onto her fork. I thought about her dating if and when Dad died. The thought caused an actual pain to burst in my chest, right where my heart was. I looked at Jess. It must be different for him, though; his father was so terrible. Surely he would be glad to see his mom dating other men.

Mom spoke again, "The truth is that I bet this is even harder for Caris to be going on a date right now than it is for you. I mean, imagine going out on your first date after all these years of being married." Mom's voice cracked, and she held her napkin up to her mouth. An uneasy silence fell over the table as Dad wrapped his arm around her shoulders. It was absolutely impossible for me to take my eyes off my parents. I watched carefully as Dad stroked Mom's hair, and she buried her forehead into his chin. They were like two pieces of a puzzle; they fit together perfectly. How would Mom ever be able to be with another man?

I felt the beating of my heart grow more rapid, and it became difficult to breathe.

Eventually Mom lifted her head and asked with a forced smile, "Gemma, did you see Trace today?"

I felt embarrassed that my entire family including Jess knew all about my crush on Trace. Was I really that much of an open book? I ducked my head as I answered, "Yes, but I think he likes Drew, so it doesn't really matter."

Everyone at the table continued eating quietly. Mom was the only one to respond. "I'm sorry, honey."

"It's okay. I never expected him to like me anyway. He's way out of my league."

"Oh, that is such bull crap," Bridget spat.

We all looked at her speechless, waiting for an explanation.

"Look at yourself in the mirror, Gemma. I don't care how inexperienced and self-doubting you are. You have this perfect little body and this shiny long brown hair that somehow wisps perfectly around your face whenever the slightest breeze blows past you." She tucked her own short hair behind her ears and stabbed at a piece of meat with her fork. "If I notice it, you can bet your pants that the boys at your school notice it."

We all sat in complete shock looking at Bridget, trying to figure out if that was a compliment or an insult.

Jess was the first one to speak, "See, Gemma? Bridget is the toughest critique out there. If you can impress her, you got it made."

Bridget cringed and fidgeted in her seat. "I never said I was *impressed*."

"Jess," Mom said as she redirected the conversation, "your mom told me you are going to California for the summer. When do you leave?"

I jerked my head at Jess. "What? You're going?" Then I paused as the reality of a Jess-less summer unfolded before me. My chest felt heavy and my eyes began to burn as I stared at Jess with angry eyes. "And you didn't tell me?"

Jess looked at the rest of my awkwardly staring family while he wiped at his mouth with a napkin and swallowed the food in his mouth. "Gemma," he whispered, "let's talk about this later."

I turned back to Mom. "How long have *you* known?"

Mom's mouth was gaping. "I'm sorry, I just assumed that Jess had told you."

"How long?" I asked again.

Mom looked at Jess with apologetic eyes while searching for the right thing to say.

Then Bridgett entered the conversation. "Well I've known for at least a week and I couldn't care less, so ... " She shrugged her shoulders apathetically and continued eating her food.

I couldn't say a word. I couldn't look at my family, who had known all this time that Jess was leaving and hadn't thought to say a word about it to me. And I definitely couldn't look at Jess, who hadn't had the decency to tell me himself. I got up from the table and without saying a word I walked out the front door and into the dark night. I kept walking down the porch steps and across the front lawn until the lights from my house no longer lit up the air around me.

I heard my front door slam, and soon rapid footsteps were coming up behind me. "Gemma!" It was Jess, and as mad at him as I was, I still couldn't help but want to turn into his arms. But I didn't. My pride wouldn't let me. So I kept walking, my arms stiff and angry at my sides. Soon Jess caught up to me and grabbed me gently on my arm. "Gemma, listen to me."

I stopped and glared at him in the darkness. I wanted to hurt him as badly as he had hurt me.

He caught his breath and continued, "I wanted to tell you ... "

"So why *didn't* you?" I spat.

"Because I knew you'd be upset. You were dealing with so much already between your dad and this Trace thing ... "

I laughed angrily. "*Trace?* You didn't tell me because of *Trace?*"

"You've just been really preoccupied lately and—"

"Don't you *dare* blame this on me! I wasn't preoccupied with Trace!" I lifted both of my arms in exasperation. "Jess, you mean *everything* to me! Who cares about *Trace?* He doesn't matter! What matters is that you are going to be three thousand miles away!"

"It's only for three months, Gemma. It's not that big of a deal."

You know when you're a little kid and you fall off something like the monkey bars or the trampoline, and after the initial hit you can't breathe for a second; you literally can't catch your breath because it's completely knocked out of you? Well, that's exactly what happened to me, right then, when Jess said that being away from me for three months wasn't that big of a deal.

I stepped away from him slowly, my body aching with the realization that he meant a whole lot more to me than I was ever going to mean to him. My jaw tightened as I turned back to the dark road. "You're right," I whispered with a raw voice. "It's not that big of a deal." I let my arm slip out of Jess's grasp and I walked away. This time he didn't follow.

chapter twenty-one

That Friday night Mom dropped me off in front of Drew's house at a quarter past eight. When I knocked on the door a woman that introduced herself as Drew's mom let me in. She was the exact opposite of what I pictured Drew's mom to be. She was small like Drew, but she had bleached blonde hair and tan skin. She looked exactly like the cheerleaders in every movie I had ever seen. She directed me to the door leading down to the finished basement. As soon as I began descending the carpeted staircase, I could hear sounds of laughter and music coming from the room that I was headed toward. My breath became shallow as I took the final step into the basement. Directly in front of me was a big-screen TV and a long leather sectional sofa. Drew was sitting cross-legged at the far end of the couch. Kit Walker was next to her, and next to him were Carmen and Stella. Then there was Trace, and to his left was Stephanie. Next to Stephanie was a boy named J.R. that I had never talked to before, but I knew him from school. And next to J.R. was his cousin, Danny, who I knew equally as well. I couldn't help but notice that there were four girls and four boys. I wondered if Drew secretly hoped I wouldn't have come.

"Gemma!" Drew called and waved me over to the couch. "Come sit down! There's a spot next to J.R."

As I walked toward my assigned seat, I made eye contact with Trace. I lifted my chin toward him to which he lifted a couple of his fingers in a half wave. He looked exceptionally good in his midnight blue button-up shirt and some long, baggy, khaki pants. His hair was doing this kind of gelled, loopy thing on top, and he looked tanner than usual on his face and neck. He was just as good looking and witty as Jess. But he was also new and exciting.

"Let's play a game." It was J.R.'s cousin Danny who said it, but we were all relieved that he did.

"Let's play Pictionary," suggested Stella.

"No. I'm a terrible drawer," complained Carmen.

"I have a game," Drew said with mischievous eyes. Everyone looked at her and waited for the name of her game.

"It's called Kissing Rugby. My brother plays it with his friends all the time."

J.R. clapped his hands together. "I vote for Drew's game."

"What's Kissing Rugby?" Stephanie asked.

Drew pointed to the back of the basement, where there was no furniture. "Everyone needs to sit on the floor. Let's go over there; there will be more room."

One by one everyone started getting up from the couch and making their way to the other side of the basement as directed. As I made my way over, I felt warm hands on my shoulders. I turned around to see Trace standing so close to me that I could have counted his eyelashes. "Hey," he said softly.

I could feel my face turn a bright shade of red. The same butterflies that always fluttered in my stomach when Trace was around were going wild. "Hi!" I forced myself to sound as perky and unaffected by him as possible.

"I was worried that you weren't going to show."

I bit my bottom lip. "My sister told me I had to be a little late or else I'd look like an idiot. She read it in some book."

Trace squinted his eyes at me. "I'm pretty sure you would have looked as good fifteen minutes ago as you do now, but either way, I'm happy to see you."

The room spun around me as I took in what he had just said. Did he just tell me that I look good? And he's happy to see me? I obviously loved hearing that, but I couldn't help but think of Jess. There was something so different about the way I felt when Jess stood this close to me. Trace was lacking the protective influence that made me feel invincible when I was with Jess. And when Jess was standing that close to me, there was no way I was thinking about Trace. When Jess stood that close to me, the rest of the world went out of focus. I shook my head at the thought of Jess and reminded myself that it didn't matter. *He isn't that big of a deal, Gemma. Remember?*

When we were all situated and sitting in a circle, Drew passed two bowls around while announcing that the girls should take one of the folded pieces of paper from the white bowl and the boys from the black bowl. We all did what we were told. I unfolded my piece of paper to see the number nine written in Drew's handwriting. I leaned toward Trace, who was sitting between Drew and me, and he showed me that his paper had the letter *Q*. "What is this about?" he asked as he showed me his letter.

I shrugged, and we both looked to Drew for an explanation.

"Okay, does everyone have a number or a letter?" she asked the group. Everyone nodded. "Here's how it works," Drew continued, holding up two other bowls, one black, one white like the others. "Each of these bowls contains the same numbers and letters that I had you all pick. So for the first round I'll pick one letter and one number out of each bowl. The person with the letter read will chase the person with the number read around the circle and so on."

"Like duck-duck-goose!" Kit shouted.

"Kind of like that, yeah," Drew replied. "Only, when you catch the person you are chasing you have to tackle them and kiss them."

"Before they sit back down in their spot," J.R. concluded.

Drew nodded. "If you get kissed, you are the chaser the next round, and we'll pick out of the bowl someone for you to chase. If the chaser doesn't catch his target, he has to go again with someone new. Got it?"

Everyone nodded, and the girls in the circle straightened their blouses and checked their hair.

Drew picked a piece of paper out of the black bowl—the boy's bowl—first. "R," she said as she looked around the circle for the boy belonging to that letter. J.R. stood up. "That's me," he said while rubbing his hands together. "All right, Drew, tell me who I'm kissing!" Everyone knew that J.R. came from a rich family. His dad was the president of some big company like Crest toothpaste or something like that. He was dressed in designer clothes from head to foot, but besides that he was kind of funny looking.

He had a small, pointy face with black curly hair that twirled around his ears. But he hung with the cool kids in school, and I could tell from the looks on the girls' faces that they wouldn't mind having their number called.

Drew pulled out the next piece of paper. "Number nine."

I gasped when I heard my number called. I looked at Trace, who urged me to stand up. "Maybe you should start with someone else," I said to Drew. "I don't even know what to do."

Drew looked pleased. "If I were you I'd start running."

From the corner of my eye, I saw J.R. inching around the circle toward me. I was absolutely positive that he was disappointed that my number was called and not one of the beautiful and popular girls that still sat in the circle. But he came toward me anyway, and so I did what I had to do. I got up and I ran. When I picked up my pace, so did J.R. I was two people away from making it back to my seat on the carpet when I felt J.R. grab hold of my arm. I yelped in fear, excitement, and anxiety—as he pulled me to the ground. I covered my face in nervous laughter as J.R. kissed me on the back of my head.

"There!" he said, pulling himself off me. He walked back to his place and sat down. "I kissed her."

I scrambled to my feet, feeling a little bit ridiculous, and looked at all the staring eyes.

"He didn't kiss her on the lips!" Kit shouted.

"I think he kissed her hair," said Stella.

"Drew never said I had to kiss her on the lips!" J.R. fought back. "She just said I had to kiss her, and I did!"

I felt so stupid. J.R. obviously didn't want to kiss me, and everyone knew it. I wanted to take off up the stairs and run home.

But I didn't; I just stood there and waited for another letter to be called out.

"J.R.'s right," Drew said as she pulled a piece of paper from the black bowl. "You just have to kiss them. It doesn't matter where." She unfolded the paper and read the letter out loud, "P."

I have to admit, I was disappointed when it wasn't Trace's letter Q, but I was even more disappointed when I saw Danny stand up with his yellowish teeth and zit-covered chin. Because Danny was J.R.'s cousin, he was invited to these types of parties by blood relation only. That's why he got away with his bad breath, hairy neck, and tapered, washed-out jeans. When his number was called, he was on his feet and running before I realized what was happening. It finally donned on me that I was supposed to chase him, and I began to clumsily sprint around the circle. I didn't even get close to him before he slid back into his original spot on the floor.

Drew took an exaggerated breath. She was obviously annoyed. "You know, Gemma, you're just going to have to keep running around the circle until you kiss someone."

I looked at her with earnest eyes. "Maybe we should let someone else have a turn."

Drew cocked her head to the side. "Gemma, it's not like this counts as your first kiss or anything. I told you that you can kiss them wherever. It doesn't have to be on the lips."

I stood in shock with the realization that Drew had just announced to everyone in the room that I had never been kissed. I could feel Trace looking up at me, but I didn't want to look back at him. I couldn't bear to look him in the eyes. I just nodded slowly at Drew as she read off the next letter, "E." Kit stood up and started galloping around the circle like he was on a pretend horse. Everyone started hooting and hollering for Kit. So I did what I had to do. I started chasing him, and I ran fast. I ran as fast as I could so that I could finally sit down and get out of this horrible predicament. Kit was barely halfway around the circle before I caught up to him, took hold of his hand, and slammed a kiss on his pinky knuckle.

"There!" I said breathlessly. "I got him." And I plopped back down onto the carpet next to Trace.

Drew didn't look impressed, but she shrugged and pulled out a number from the white bowl. The game continued on. Boys chasing girls, girls chasing boys. Most of the kisses were given somewhere on the head or cheek or even nose. No one had gone straight for the lips yet, though I swear Kit tried to kiss Drew on the lips, but she turned her head before he got the chance. As time went on, the tackling was more athletic, the hollering from the rest of us in the circle was louder, and everyone knew everyone's number so we all knew exactly what number or letter to wish for when it was our turn to chase or be chased. Trace had just been chased, tackled, and kissed on the ear by Stella, who was a lot more aggressive than I ever would have guessed, leaving Trace standing and waiting for the number to be called out of the girl he was supposed to chase.

Drew pulled a piece of paper from the white bowl. Maybe it was just my imagination, but I swear I saw the number five—Stephanie's number—through the white paper when she unfolded it. But the number that Drew called out wasn't five. The number she called out was the number seven. It was her own number.

She threw the bowl of papers down on the ground and made a whoop sound as she took off running around the circle. Trace took off chasing her. A sickening feeling grew in my stomach as I thought about watching him kiss her. I wanted to close my eyes. But I couldn't. I just watched the horrific scene unfold before me. But as I watched I realized it wasn't all that horrific after all. In fact, Trace was barely moving. His run was more like an injured looking jog, and he made no real attempt to reach for her even when she slowed down to let him catch her. Before long they had made their way around the circle and Drew was back at her original spot. All she could do was sit down. She had beat him. She was victorious. Or was she? I watched her closely. She was breathing heavily and smiling slightly as she picked up the bowl and the papers that had fallen out. "I knew you couldn't catch me," she said, waving her hand at Trace. But there was an awkward silence from the crowd. A silence that made me realize that everyone knew the truth. Everyone knew that Trace hadn't given it his all.

Drew quickly pulled another number out of the white bowl. She looked at the unfolded piece of paper for a long moment before reading it out loud. "Gemma," she looked up at me and stared emotionlessly into my eyes. "It's you. Number nine."

I acted as normal as I could as I got up from my spot and took off running around the circle. I was paying less attention to the game at hand and more attention to Drew when I was suddenly tackled to the ground by the huge force behind me. It was, of course, Trace, and he ruthlessly pinned me down underneath him. He hovered over me with a red face and a wide smile and then began leaning down toward me in slow motion. I held my breath, waiting for him to kiss me and wondering where he was going to do it. My cheek? My forehead? But as he leaned closer, he was looking straight at my lips. His eyes were zeroed in on them as if they were the elk and he was the hunter. My breath was caught in my throat as I quickly licked my lips. There wasn't a sound in the room besides Trace's breathing. And in the next moment, it was happening. Trace's lips made contact with mine. I closed my eyes, and my mind went blank. I had no idea what to do so I just lay there and let him kiss me. Trace's lips pressed firmly against mine for a second or two before he pulled slowly away and sat back on his heels.

The group erupted in cheering as Trace helped me up off the ground. "I hope that was okay," Trace whispered as he smoothed out my hair.

I pulled on my shirt and rubbed at my frazzled hair as I nodded politely at him. "Sure, it's a game. That's how you play it, I guess." But the truth was that I felt angry, disgusted, and violated. He knew I had never been kissed, and yet he still did it in front of the entire group for a stupid game. My first kiss was over. I felt empty. And my lips tasted like Trace's stale gum.

"Who's next?" J.R. asked when the chatter had died down.

"No one," Drew said as she stood up onto her feet. "This game is getting lame." She walked back to the couch and sat down by herself. I looked at the clock on the wall. It was almost eleven.

"I should probably go upstairs and wait for my mom to come," I said to anyone that was listening. But everyone besides Trace was laughing at J.R.'s impression of Stella running away from Danny.

"I'll go wait with you." Trace looked into my eyes with a serious expression that made me recoil.

"It's okay," I objected. "I'm sure she'll be here any minute."

Trace looked like he was going to object but decided not to after examining my expression. "I'll see you on Monday then."

"Sure, Monday," I stammered, then I turned toward the couch to say good-bye to Drew. But she wasn't there. When I reached the top of the stairs, the house was completely dark. The house looked a lot smaller tonight than it had when I was there three months ago making the movie for German class. I looked out the front window, but Mom's car was nowhere to be seen.

"No one's out there."

I jumped at the voice that came from the pitch-black living room on my left. I squinted my eyes into the dark until I saw the black shadow of Drew sitting hunched over on the piano bench.

I breathed easier. "Drew, I didn't see you there."

I thought I heard her laugh, but she didn't say anything in response.

"I looked for you downstairs to say good-bye. Why are you up here all alone?" My eyes were finally adjusting to the darkness, and I could see her more clearly as I walked into the living room.

"You know I like him. You *know* that."

I searched for something to say, something that would make me innocent in this situation, but I was coming up with nothing. "Drew, I—"

"I asked you in the beginning if you liked him."

"I know," I said quietly.

"Did you not like him then? Did you only start liking him after I told you that I liked him?" Drew sounded more hurt than angry.

"I don't know." I felt like a child as I searched for an answer. "I've liked him for a long time. But I had just barely started hanging out with you. I had made the mistake before of telling friends who I liked just to have them use it against me."

"Sounds familiar," Drew spoke softly, but her words dug into my chest like a dagger.

I had no idea how to respond so I just stood in the darkness completely quiet.

Drew filled the silence. "You want to know what's ironic? I actually started liking Jess more than Trace. But when I saw the way you lit up whenever Jess's name was mentioned, I decided to stay away from him."

Right then Mom's car lights flashed across the front windows. I stood motionless for a moment longer watching Drew's black figure in the darkness. Then I turned to the door and left, without saying a word.

An hour later I was staring at myself in the bathroom mirror with toothpaste foaming out the corners of my mouth. My skin looked flushed, and the mascara that I had carefully applied to my eyelashes earlier that night had rubbed off leaving me looking three years younger than I wanted to look. How had I ended up in this place? Jess didn't care about me the way I wanted him to. Trace had just taken away my first kiss. And Drew, the only girl that I had ever really liked hanging out with, hated me because I hypothetically stabbed her in the back. I turned on the water faucet and spat into the sink. I watched as my pasted saliva swirled around and around and eventually slid down the drain. I thought about Trace and the way his chapped lips had stayed pressed against mine while everybody stared. I thought about Drew hunched over her piano in the dark as she asked me questions that I didn't have the answer to. I thought about Jess and how easily he had loosened his grip on my arm as I walked away from him that night on the street. And I couldn't help but feel that my life at the moment felt a whole lot like that downward swirling string of spit.

chapter twenty-two

"*Uh, this is kind of* awkward." I was at my locker the next Monday morning before school when I suddenly felt Trace's breath on the back of my neck. "But you're at the wrong locker."

I breathed in a heavy sigh and turned around to face him. He looked so perfect, especially for seven forty in the morning. He had fresh gum in his mouth, and his lips were just slightly parted with a bit of a smile as he spoke. Yet somehow my stomach didn't flutter—not one bit—as he looked humorously into my eyes. "Your locker is actually in the elementary school a few blocks down the road."

I bit my lip as an effort to smile at his joke, but I had too much on my mind to actually find it funny. "Trace," I said before I could talk myself out of it, "you didn't ask me to dance last year at the Valentine's dance."

Trace's lips fell as he took in what I was saying.

I continued with a nervous laugh, "You probably don't even remember this, but my friends Clarissa and Nina asked you ... "

"I remember." Trace hugged his arms around his chest and narrowed his eyes as he spoke, "Of course I remember that."

"So why are you paying all of this attention to me when you obviously don't like me?"

"Who said I don't like you?"

I threw my hands up in the air. "You didn't ask me to dance, Trace! If you liked me you would have asked me to dance!"

"I was planning on asking you dance." He leaned closer to me with a sense of urgency in his voice. "It took me a minute to find you, okay? But by the time I did find you, you were already dancing with Jess Tyler."

I swallowed as I recalled that day. I supposed I hadn't given Trace much time before practically leaping into Jess's arms. "You could have cut in," I said flatly.

"And take you away from Jess Tyler?" Trace shook his head. "I watched you two together that day. There was something going on there."

"Maybe there was," I said gloomily, "but not anymore."

I couldn't believe it was already the end of May. There were only a few days left of my junior high career. Soon I was going to be in tenth grade. Soon I was going to be a high-school student. The thought of it was surreal. It was what I had been waiting for all year and yet I just couldn't bring myself to get excited about it. Jess was leaving—sometime—I hadn't talked to him since that night in front of my house, which meant I had no idea when he was heading out to California for the summer. It also meant that he didn't know anything about Trace kissing me, or my fight with Drew, or anything that had happened to me for the past few weeks. It felt strange and lonely. I hated it. It wasn't that Jess hadn't tried to make contact with me. He had called a few times and he even threw rocks at my window one night. But I ignored him. Why should I care about him when he obviously didn't care about me?

I wasn't talking to Drew either. Or maybe she wasn't talking to me. I wasn't sure anymore. I noticed in German class that she always sat alone in the back. Carmen, Stella, and Stephanie sat on the opposite side of the room, and Trace usually found a seat somewhere around me. I liked talking to Trace, and it was great to have someone to walk with through the halls, but despite what everyone in our class was thinking, we were just friends.

It was almost noon on the last day of school. The halls were mostly empty since everyone was let out early to go sign year-books on the soccer field. I was running late though, mostly because I still hadn't cleaned out my locker and partly because I didn't know who I would possibly ask to sign my yearbook.

I was walking through the halls with my hands full of old notebooks and a few pop cans that I had just scoured from my locker. I was sauntering slowly past the lockers, soaking in my last day as a junior high student when I noticed a familiar shadow at the end of the hall. It was Drew, and she was at her locker. She was squatting on the ground, stuffing the last of her things into her backpack when she turned to the sound of my footsteps echoing in the hall.

"Hi," I said as I approached her. I stopped next to her locker and waited to see how she would respond.

She stood up slowly and looked me in the eyes. "Hey."

"Can I ask you a question?"

Drew bit the side of her cheek as she considered it. Eventually she nodded.

"Why did you become friends with me?"

Drew folded her arms. "Truthfully?"

"That would be nice."

She watched me carefully as though trying to determine whether I could handle what she was about to tell me. She stood perfectly still, barely moving her lips when she said, "You looked lonely."

I pitched my head forward in shock. "Lonely?"

Drew shrugged her shoulders. "I thought you could use a friend."

Nothing she could have said would have surprised me more than that. I had always looked at Drew as a selfish person–there always had to be something in it for her. For the first time ever, I felt like I was seeing the real Drew. And it was answering a lot of questions. It explained why she had been so insistent on me sharing her locker with her even though there was barely enough room for my notebook. It explained why she wanted to throw a party with so many people at my house. It may have even explained why she stopped being my friend when the party was a bust.

I watched Drew as she picked up her heavy backpack and shut her locker one last time. I was sad that I had let so much time go without knowing the truth about her.

Drew started walking down the hall and then paused to see if I was going to follow. When I fell in stride beside her she asked, "What are you doing this summer?"

The thought of summer made my heart ache. "Not much. You?"

"I'll be at my dad's in Atlanta."

"Oh yeah." She had told me that back in March when we were friends on a daily basis.

"You'll probably hang out with Jess, right?"

I sighed heavily, "No. He's going to California."

"California? Why?"

"Same reason as you, to be with his dad."

"I didn't know his parents were divorced. He always seemed like he had a perfect life."

"I don't think anybody has a perfect life," I responded. I opened the door that led outside, and we both stepped out into the sunshine. "Are you going to the yearbook signing?"

Drew squinted into the light. "I don't think there's any point. I can't think of one person who would want to sign my yearbook."

"I know what you mean."

Drew looked up at me and with a hint of hesitation asked, "Do you want to come over to my house?"

I was caught off guard by her invitation but somehow not all that surprised. "I would, but I promised my mom I'd be home this afternoon to help her with some stuff."

Drew pursed her lips and looked down at the ground beneath us. "Well, I guess I'll see you next year?"

"Maybe we can be locker partners."

Drew bit her lip and nodded. "That would be good." She shot me a half smile before turning toward the road that led to her house. I watched her as she walked away, and as I did I thought about the past few months since we had become friends. We went through a lot in that time, and I figured if we had made it that far, maybe our friendship was stronger than I thought.

I turned the opposite way and headed toward mine and Jess's

shortcut home. Even though he hadn't been there to walk it with me for an entire year, in my mind, it would always belong to both of us. I made my way across our old soccer field, through our hole in the fence, and around our concrete jungle. It seemed so much smaller now than it used to. I sat for a while on our block wall and looked out over our trees and our lake. And as I made my last steps home on my last day in junior high, I felt a little bit older, a little bit more mature, and a little bit more comfortable in my bra.

chapter
twenty-three

My heart was pounding as I approached my house because sitting on the front porch in his usual spot on the steps was Jess. It had been a week since he had made any attempts to talk to me, and there he was again as if no time had passed. I had about ten seconds of walking before I reached him to be able to decide what I was going to do with the situation. I missed him terribly. The biggest part of me wanted to run to him, let him wrap his arms around me, and tell him all about my day. But a smaller part of me—the much more prideful part of me—wanted to do the opposite. The prideful part of me won.

"What are you doing here?" I asked callously when I was within a couple feet of him.

Jess pulled himself to standing and stuck both of his hands deep in his jean pockets. "I just wanted to say goodbye," he replied. His eyes were turned down at the corners, and I thought he looked a bit pale.

"When are you leaving?" I was dying to know, but I shielded my emotions by speaking as flatly as I possibly could.

"Tonight."

His answer stung my ears and the tips of my toes. But I shrugged my shoulders and walked passed him up the stairs. "Have a nice summer."

"Gemma." Jess's voice was firm as he called after me.

I turned around when I reached the top of the porch. "What?"

"Why are you *so* mad at me? You haven't talked to me in weeks. Is this really all because I didn't tell you I was going to California?"

It was a valid question. One I had thought about many times since that night on the street. I was hurt that he hadn't told me, but no, that wasn't why I was angry. I was angry at him for not caring. I was angry at him for not wanting me the same way I wanted him. But I didn't say that. Instead I said, "It really doesn't matter. I've hardly thought about it."

Jess lifted his chin and stepped backward toward the lawn. "Really, that's good. I was afraid you were mad."

"I've had a lot going on so ..." I waved my hand at a bug as my lie floated away with the breeze.

Jess nodded and puffed out his bottom lip. "How are things going anyway, with Drew and Trace and all that?"

I faked a smile. "Trace kissed me at that party." I leaned against the porch railing. "It was just a game, but no one else got kissed on the lips."

Jess flexed his jaw and looked down at the grass. "Sounds like things are working out for you then."

No, not at all actually. I didn't even like the kiss. I wish it had never happened. I wish the person who kissed me was you. "Yeah, I guess."

Jess looked at the house behind me, then at the ground again, then at a nearby tree. He couldn't look me in the eye. He hated me for letting Trace kiss me. He always said I was too immature for stuff like that. And now he couldn't stand to look at me.

"Well I got to go," Jess said as he backed away farther toward the sidewalk. "I need to pack still."

I turned toward my house and opened the front door. I spoke to the doorknob as I muttered, "Have a good trip."

I stepped through the door and closed it behind me, but just before it shut I heard his soft voice say, "Bye, Gemma."

The pizza guy came that night at six o'clock. Mom was out to dinner with my aunt that was in town from Albuquerque, and Bridget was on a date, so Dad ordered pizza and we ate it together on the couch while watching some old cowboy movie that made him feel like a kid again. I was bored with the movie, but I loved spending time with Dad—just the two of us. On the screen in front of me some cowboys were tromping through the desert on horseback looking for Indians, but my thoughts were with Jess and the horrible way I had let things end.

"What you thinking about?" Dad asked.

I waved my hand at the television with a smirk. "Cowboys and Indians, obviously."

Dad pointed the remote control at the screen and hit pause. "Come on, what's on your mind?"

I scowled at the piece of hair I was twisting between my fingers. "Jess."

"When does he leave for California?"

"Tonight sometime." I looked out the window toward his house. It was starting to get dark. "He could be gone already."

"Did you say goodbye?"

"I guess." I slouched into the couch. "Things between Jess and me are just…" I paused to think of the right word, "confusing."

Dad let his head rest on the back of the couch. He was looking better these days, but he was still tired. "What's so confusing about it? You two are best friends. You love being together. What more do you need to know?"

I looked at Dad from the corner of my eye. I had never admitted to anyone that I had feelings for Jess. But there was something about the way we were sitting there together, eating pizza and watching a cowboy movie that made me want to open up to him.

"Sometimes I think I want to be more than just friends with him."

"But?" Dad asked with raised eyebrows. He wasn't surprised with my confession.

"*But* he doesn't feel the same way about me."

"How do you know?"

"I just do," I said more harshly than I meant to. Every time I talked about Jess or thought about Jess I felt rejected. I was beginning to hate the sound of his name. "Dad?" I was hoping to change the subject, though my next question was anything but easy to ask. "Are you going to die?"

Dad turned his head toward me again and took in a deep breath of air. "The doctors are giving us every reason to hope." He brushed his hand over my hair, which fell against my back. "That being said, it is possible that I will die sooner than I'd like."

I stared blankly at the paused movie in front of me while hugging my knees close to my chest. My stomach started tightening, and I felt like I wanted to throw up. "We're never going to go up to the Cape again, are we?"

He dipped his chin toward his chest. "Probably not."

I nodded my head like it wasn't a big deal. I didn't want to make him sadder than he already was.

"I know it's hard, but," he hesitated, "it's kind of like the problem you're having with Jess. Right now it seems earth shattering, like it's the end of the world. But from my point of view, I know that it's not. I know that you're only at the beginning of your story. The experiences you're having with Jess and all your friends are just life lessons for the bigger things that will come later on. And I think that it's the same with my illness. Right now the idea of dying is," he paused for a moment, "well, to be honest, it's downright terrifying. But I have faith that we don't have the whole picture. And I have faith that there's someone out there that does, and he knows that this is only the beginning. He knows that the experiences I'm having here on earth are just preparing me for the bigger things that will come later on."

"You mean, like life after death?"

"Yeah, like life after death." My parents had raised Bridget and me to believe in God and heaven, but now that it was a reality that was staring us in the face, the whole idea became more than a Sunday school lesson. It was real, and for the first time in my life I had to actually decide what I believed in. I bit my lip. "What do you think heaven is like?"

"Oh, I don't know." Dad sighed and folded his hands behind his head. "I think it's a place where there are no bills, no taxes, and no debt." He chuckled. "It makes me wonder why I'm so scared to go there."

"Maybe it's just the not knowing," I offered.

"I'm sure you're right." He brushed my hair again with his hand. "You know what I really think, though?"

"What?"

"I think heaven is just like our road trips to Cape Cod. The windows are down, The Beatles are blaring from the stereo, and you and Mom and Bridge and I are all singing at the tops of our lungs with the wind blowing through our hair." Dad lay his head back on the couch cushion and let a wide grin spread across his cheeks.

"And," I added, "there are endless fields of whistle grass." I couldn't help but think about Jess right then, and his pathetic attempts to make a sound through a blade of grass. I had thought he looked so cute that day, the sun shining in his hair. His lips puckered against his thumbs. I missed him so badly that my heart literally ached.

Dad looked up at the ceiling deep in thought then said, "You know, Gem, this thing with you and Jess ... it will all work out. Jess cares about you, and he'll be back in a few months. There's no need to rush things." Dad's eyes began to slowly close as his hands relaxed on his lap. He was tired, and I needed to let him rest.

I gathered up our plates full of uneaten pizza crusts and dropped them in the kitchen before starting up the stairs to my bedroom. I was startled when dad's voice filled the silent house once more. "That being said," he paused, and I turned on the steps to wait for him to continue, "life is short, and if you don't let Jess know how you feel about him, the moment might pass you by."

chapter
twenty-four

I threw myself on top of my bed and stared at the ceiling as my dad's last words pressed against my brain. Let him know how I feel? I thought it was the boy's job to do that. What would I say to him? Would I really just walk right up to him and tell him I liked him as more than a friend? And what would he say if I did? What if he laughed at me? What if he told me to get real? Maybe I should just forego all talking and go straight for the kiss. But what if I was bad at it? What if he pulled away and disgustedly wiped off his mouth? What if it made things so awkward and so horrible between us that we could never be friends again? I kicked my shoes off the side of the bed and pulled the comforter up to my knees. Who was I kidding? I wasn't going to go over there and tell him how I felt. And I definitely wasn't going to walk straight up to him and kiss him. I didn't even know if he was home. For all I knew he was already gone and I wouldn't see him again for three months. I squeezed the bracelet he gave me between my fingers. But if he was so disgusted by me why did he always stand so close? And why did he always seem to get lost in my eyes? I thought about Jess when he got to California, all tan with bleached hair, walking along the ocean somewhere. What if he met someone there? Some beach girl with a big chest and perfect white teeth. What if he fell in love with her and never forgot her? What if she became the girl that he always thought about? What if Dad was right? What if this was my last chance to tell him how I felt? I sat up and twisted myself around until my feet were dangling off the side of my bed. I stared at my shoes then nudged them slightly with the tip of my big toe. What if I was changing my life forever by sitting here in bed, doing nothing?

"I'll be right back, Dad!" I shouted as I jumped over the last step of the staircase and breezed past my dad. He was watching the cowboy movie again, and he lifted his arm and yelled, "Good luck!" as I flew out the door.

I stared up at Jess's big, dark house as I tiptoed around to the backyard. The window to his room was lit, and a spark of excitement filled my chest. I picked up a handful of small rocks and lobbed one at his window. I missed. I threw another one that smacked against the glass. The curtains behind the window fluttered, and soon Jess's sister, Vivian, appeared through the open glass. "You again," she said smugly. "Don't you know you could break the window?"

"Can you go get Jess?" I said with urgency in my voice.

She curled her lips. "He's not here. He and my mom left for the airport ten minutes ago."

Her words fell on top of me like a load of bricks. I had just barely missed him. I hopelessly stepped backward and turned into the darkness. "He left you a letter, though." I jerked around at this new bit of information. Vivian disappeared into the room then came back with a folded up piece of lined paper in her left hand. "He asked me to give it to you. Here." She dropped the paper out the window, and it fluttered down to my feet. I picked it up and muttered, "Thanks." I left Jess's house and walked down the street to the concrete jungle. I pulled myself up onto our usual wall and unfolded Jess's letter. The sun had been down for a while now, but there was still enough light in the hazy gray sky for me to make out the words on the paper in front of me.

Gem,

There's so much I want to tell you that I have never had the guts to say out loud. First of all, I'm sorry I didn't tell you sooner that I was leaving for the summer. When I found out I had to leave—it was the worst news I could think of. I didn't want to go to California. I didn't want to have to live with my dad all summer. And I didn't want to leave home. I guess I thought that the longer I went without saying it out loud, without seeing your reaction, the less it would hurt. But I was wrong. Because it's not the saying it out loud that hurts. It's not even your reaction that hurts the most. The thing that hurts the most, that makes it hard to sleep at night, is not being with you.

Second, when you first told me that Trace kissed you I was so mad. Not because you had your first kiss, because you're beautiful and you deserve to have your first kiss with a guy that you like. But because the honest truth of the matter is—I was hoping that I would be your first kiss. And even more truthfully, I've always sort of hoped that I would also be your last kiss. There, I said it (or wrote it, actually) but

it's out there and now that you've read this far into the letter I'm worried that you are disgusted by what I've said and
won't ever want to talk to me again. But this is written in
pen so I can't erase it now.

And lastly, the past three weeks that I haven't been able to
see you and talk to you have been the longest three weeks
of my life. So if this letter freaks you out in any way let's
just forget about it. We can just be friends. I can handle the
rejection, I can keep my true feelings to myself, but I can't
stand to not have you in my life.

Your Best Friend (and secretly more),

Jess

I took in a deep breath and tried to recover from the gush
of confessions. I squeezed the letter between my fingers and
scanned it once more with glistening eyes. Had he really written those words? Was it true that he secretly wanted to be *more*
than just my best friend? I brought the letter up to my nose and
breathed in its scent. Even the paper smelled like Jess. My heart
ached to have him on the wall next to me, his arm around me, his
eyes gently watching me. But he was gone, and there was nothing
I could do but spend the long, hot summer alone, waiting for him
to come home.

I folded the letter back up and gently slid it into my jeans
pocket. The night was humid, and my clothes and hair were
sticking to my warm skin as I made my way off the cement wall.
I looked up at the dark sky. Thick gray clouds blocked my view
from the stars. It was going to rain. I tried to picture Jess in
my mind. What was he doing? What was he thinking? I had no
way to get a hold of him. No way to tell him that the kiss with

Trace meant nothing. That the only one I ever really wanted was him. I stepped into the street and thought about that day—so long ago—when I thought I heard Jess say that he loved me. Had I heard him correctly? Had he been feeling this way for that long? I felt a raindrop on my nose. As I wiped it away, a clap of thunder crashed against the sky. The smell of a summer storm filled the air, and a million tiny rain drops began tapping the ground around me. I grasped my ruby in my hand, the ruby that was supposedly the most powerful gem in the world—like me, he had said, and like us. Were we really that strong? Were these feelings we had for each other powerful enough to carry us through the summer? I reached into my pocket and caressed Jess's letter with my fingertips. Would he still feel the same way when he returned? Was I ever going to feel his lips against mine?

The rain was pouring hard now. I shielded my head with both of my arms as I sprinted the rest of the way to my house and across the front lawn. I was nearly to the safety of my front porch when I heard a voice through the sheets of rain.

"Gemma?" I knew the voice perfectly, but still I doubted. It couldn't possibly be him. He had left for the airport. He was probably halfway there by now. How could he possibly be here, in my front yard, saying my name?

I turned to the voice, and though my eyes were blurred by the puddles of water building up around my cheeks, I saw him standing there—not ten feet away from me. He was soaking wet and holding a handful of small rocks. And his face was full of vulnerability.

I was wet through by now, but I didn't notice. I didn't notice the thunder or the wind whipping my wet hair against my neck.

The only thing I could see, the only thing that mattered, was Jess in his worn out blue jeans and his dripping wet T-shirt.

"I thought you were gone," I yelled over the roaring sounds of the storm. I pointed at his house behind me. "I went to your window…"

But there was no time to finish. Because while I was talking and pointing and explaining, Jess was coming toward me, one step at a time, his eyes locked with mine. It happened so quickly, and yet I captured every moment. His warm hands as they cupped my cold, wet cheeks. The curve of his left forearm as I grasped it with one hand while placing the other on his drenched chest. The delicious smell of his breath as he moved in without hesitation. And the creamy taste of his lips as they found their place perfectly between the crevices of my own. The thunder crashed around us. The lightning filled the darkened sky. Water streamed down our cheeks and off our noses and between our lips as we savored this final moment that we had together.

When the time came for us to separate—not because we wanted to but because we absolutely had to—Jess opened his eyes with his hands still holding my face and said softly, "Viv called and said you came over." He closed his eyes and pressed his forehead against mine. "It made me hope."

I wrapped my arms around his torso and pulled him toward me. I knew he was going to have to leave soon if he was going to make his flight. As hard as it was to let him go before the kiss, now it was a million times harder. But as we stood in the rain, holding onto each other with no intentions of letting go, I had to think of Dad's words from earlier that evening. As devastating as it was going to be to have to release my hold on Jess and let him drive away for the next three months, I knew that this wasn't the end. I knew that this was only the beginning of our story.

Some hours after Jess and I had given each other a hundred final kisses goodbye, I climbed into my soft, warm bed with dry pajamas on and my wet hair pulled into a ponytail. I longed to hear the tapping of a rock at my window. But I knew it wouldn't come. I ached to feel Jess's lips against mine just one more time. But I had to be grateful that I had felt that at all. I pulled my comforter up to my chin and stared out the window at the now clear sky. The summer storm had blown over, and from where I was lying I could see a thousand tiny, sparkling stars. After all that had happened—the big things and the small, the good and the bad—I finally fell asleep to the quiet and perfect memory of not my first, but my second kiss.

DATE DUE

DEC 1 8 2016		

PRINTED IN U.S.A.